Dragons of Wind and Waves

DRAGONS OF WIND AND WAVES

DRAGONS OF EARTH, WATER, FIRE AND AIR

To Kamryn
Happy Reading!
Susan Brown

BY

SUSAN BROWN

YELLOW FARMHOUSE PUBLICATIONS

Dragons of Wind and Waves

ISBN-13: 978-1727095531
ISBN-10: 1727095537

Yellow Farmhouse Publications, Lake Stevens, WA, USA

Publication Date: September 2018

Design: Heather McIntyre
Cover&Layout, www.coverandlayout.com

Cover Photography: Waves © NeuPaddy;
Clouds © FocusEditzDeba

For my wonderful daughters,
Laurel, Heather, and Karen
who have helped me,
put up with me, and never
stopped cheering me on.

OTHER BOOKS BY SUSAN BROWN YOU MIGHT ENJOY

Dragons of Earth, Water, Fire, and Air

Dragons of Frost and Fire

Dragons of Desert and Dust

A Thunder of Dragons

New! Boxed Set includes *Dragons of Frost and Fire, Dragons of Desert and Dust, Dragons of Wind and Waves, A Thunder of Dragons*

For Teens:

Hey, Chicken Man!

Not Yet Summer

Sammy and the Devil Dog

With Anne Stephenson:

Something's Fishy at Ash Lake

An Amber & Elliot Mystery

The Mad Hacker

An Amber & Elliot Mystery (Fall 2018)

Written with Anne Stephenson as Stephanie Browning

Outbid by the Star

Undone by the Boss

Making Up is Hard to Do

Short Story Collections:

Holiday Cheers: *Stories to Celebrate Your Year*

Romance in Pajama Pants: *Stories to Celebrate Your Happily Ever After*

Coming Soon:

Catching Toads

You're Dead, David Borelli

Dragons of
Wind and Waves

CONTENTS

ONE: *STORM-SHADOWED*	ADDIE
TWO: *THIS WON'T END WELL*	JACOB
THREE: *NOT SCARED*	MARGO
FOUR: *NORMAL*	ADDIE
FIVE: *SAPPHIRE*	JACOB
SIX: *DRAGON SLAYER*	MARGO
SEVEN: *STORMS AND SECRETS*	ADDIE
EIGHT: *NIGHTMARES*	JACOB
NINE: *SILVER*	ADDIE
TEN: *THEY'VE FOUND US*	MARGO
ELEVEN: *FIND THE MAGIC*	JACOB
TWELVE: *HERE BE DRAGONS*	ADDIE
THIRTEEN: *HER FATHER'S BOOT*	MARGO
FOURTEEN: *BRING IT ON*	JACOB
FIFTEEN: *THE BRIDGE ACROSS THE ABYSS*	ADDIE
SIXTEEN: *POOLS OF BLOOD*	MARGO
SEVENTEEN: *MAGIC IS ALL WE'VE GOT!*	JACOB
EIGHTEEN: *PSYCHOTIC FIGMENTS OF IMAGINATION*	ADDIE
NINETEEN: *THE LAST WARRIOR*	MARGO
TWENTY: *WE HAVE TO GET AWAY!*	JACOB
TWENTY-ONE: *THE BLOOD ISN'T HERE*	MARGO
TWENTY-TWO: *YOU'LL PAY*	JACOB
TWENTY-THREE: *THE ENEMY COMES*	ADDIE
TWENTY-FOUR: *TIME FOR YOU TO DIE*	JACOB
TWENTY-FIVE: *THEY KNOW WE'RE COMING*	ADDIE
TWENTY-SIX: *DESTINY AND DOOM*	MARGO

TWENTY-SEVEN: *KILL THEM!* *JACOB*
TWENTY-EIGHT: *THE CIRCLE* *ADDIE*

SNEAK PEEK! DRAGONS OF DESERT AND DUST
SNEAK PEEK! DRAGONS OF FROST AND FIRE
ABOUT THE AUTHOR

ONE

STORM-SHADOWED

ADDIE

Lightning strobed across her walls. Thunder shook the windows. Addie crouched in her bed, pressing her palms against her head, as if to push back the emotions throbbing in response to this elemental chaos.

When she couldn't hold it in any longer, Addie leaped out of bed, reached for the curtains, and yanked them fully open. The storm-shadowed dawn revealed rain driven nearly sideways by wind that roiled through gaunt trees, whipping and scattering branches.

With shaking hands, Addie pushed open the window. From the nearby bluff at the end of their property, the sound of surf crashing over rocks echoed through her room until the crack and roll of advancing thunder drowned it out.

Nothing in her old city life could compare to the gales roaring inland from the Atlantic.

Nothing in her memory could compare to the frenzy rioting through her blood.

Nothing in her experience could compare to the elemental joy coursing through her spirit.

She hesitated a moment, then unable to help herself, yanked on a jacket and raced into the hall. She skidded to a halt. Her twin, Jacob, was there already, struggling into his own jacket, leaning against the doorjamb with his arm crutches half-cuffed to help support him. She should have known he would feel the awakening fever in her blood, and no matter what, would be ready to follow her.

She grinned. "Coming?"

He nodded. Together, they moved down the hall as quickly Jacob's unwieldy body would allow.

"Jacob?" Their father's sleepy voice reached them. "Everything okay?"

Addie clapped a hand over her mouth to stop her rising giggles.

"G..going to the ba..athroom, Dad," Jacob called out, his handicap as always breaking up his speech.

Nothing but soft snores replied.

"You know, th..there isn't another f..fifteen-year-old in the u..universe going out into a storm like this," he whispered.

"That's because *we* are the most amazing teens in the universe," Addie retorted.

"The m..most insane...." Jacob rolled his eyes, but gestured ahead with his crutch. Addie grinned and hurried down the hall. Behind her, Jacob's crutches made soft thuds on the worn carpet. Almost dancing with the madness, she moved only a little ahead, ready to catch him if he lost his balance on the stairs.

At the kitchen door Addie yanked on her boots, then pushed Jacob onto a chair to help jam on his.

"Good?" she asked.

"Y..yeah." His eyes gleamed in a sudden flash of lightning.

Outside, the wind blasted across the land, nearly knocking them both back into the house. Addie's heart sang at the raw power, but she grabbed Jacob's arm and together they leaned into the gale. Overhead, another crackle of lightning flared through the contorted woods. A distant tree exploded. Thunder blasted their ears.

"Th..this may not be s..safe!" Jacob shouted in her ear.

"But it's glorious," Addie answered, pulling him along the path to the bluff. "It's in our blood!"

"Our b..blood is crazy!" Jacob yelled.

The gusting wind tried to dash them onto the rocks below, but they clung to the thrashing trees. Black clouds fought their way across the sky, hurling ribbons of lightning into the heaving Atlantic. Beyond the headland, giant grey waves curled and roared. Towers of water crashed against ancient stone breakwaters, then rose again, lashed by wind into racing towards land, smashing themselves on the rocks and bluff, churning spray high into the sodden air.

Addie and Jacob were drenched. They laughed breathlessly, sucking in the salty air, clinging to the trees, rough bark scraping their hands, driven rain stinging their faces. For long moments, they simply rocked with the trees, reveling in the power of the elements around them. Then Addie let go and, using the wind, swayed across the sodden grass.

"C..careful..." Jacob warned.

Addie gave no sign she had heard. In her mind she was being carried upward on the wind, soaring across the waves, enthralled by the bitter spray sheeting her skin. On and on, over sea and land, all the elements of the world cradling and holding her.

Then the exultation abruptly ebbed away and she crouched, shivering, on the ground.

The worst of the storm was passing, moving north along the Nova Scotia coastline, funneled toward the St. Lawrence River. Breath coming in gasps, Addie got to her feet and supported herself against a black spruce.

"I know it's crazy," she said to Jacob as the wind dropped away. "But these storms make me feel so alive." Her voice felt scratched and raw.

He nodded, tossed back his sopping hair and looked at his watch. "W..we have to get ready for s..school."

That bit of practicality struck Addie as insanely funny, and she began to laugh. Jacob only half-smiled, his own face lined with fatigue. Addie took his shaking arm and together they made their way across the rank grass, through the dripping ferns and brambles, back to the house.

Storms were her thing. Addie couldn't resist them. But Jacob had never let her face them alone, no matter how exhausting it was for him.

Inside the kitchen, she crouched, gently pulled off his boots and set them upside down on a heat register. Chances were their dad would never notice.

Since their mom had disappeared eight months ago, he never noticed anything. In a frantic frenzy, the twins' dad had moved what was left of the family to Port St. George, where he had originally met Audra Medway years before. But after uprooting them and hauling all their belongings to this old clapboard house on the bluff, Jim Medway had completely shut down. He didn't see the tiredness etching Jacob's thin face. Didn't notice how much Addie despised this town with its sagging houses, dreary general store, and gossipy, mean-spirited people who made it their business to demonstrate that they didn't much like strangers.

As she helped Jacob maneuver up the uneven staircase, Addie wondered if her dad even guessed how he and their mother had trashed their lives? Did he actually believe their mom would show up here after all this time? The high school was awful for Addie and the uneven terrain in this oceanside town was torture for Jacob. His life was hard enough without their parents messing it up even more.

Snores still drifted from their father's room. With a sigh of relief, Jacob dropped his crutches and stretched out on his bed. Addie got a towel from the hall closet, and tossed it to him.

"You can sleep for a bit," she told him. "I'm too wound up. I'll wake you in time to get ready for school."

He barely nodded before his eyes drifted shut.

Feeling a stab of guilt, Addie went back to her own room and sat at the window watching the last dregs of the storm skulking in from the ocean. She had a clear view of the bay from here, could see the steel grey water chopping over barriers, the uneven waves dropping lower and lower with each curl over the shore.

The only good thing about Port St. George, Addie thought, was the ocean and the wind-whipped storms. The kind their mother had loved. The kind that sent Addie's blood singing and boiling. The kind that made her feel how different she was from other teens.

Leaning on her elbows, Addie breathed in the salt-laden air. No matter how much she hated Port St. George and the kids she'd met, she felt more alive here than ever before – as if the gusty sea air was building muscle into her body and intelligence into her brain. If only she could bring her mom back and deport all the other residents, Addie thought, it would be about perfect.

But today was Monday and the whole damn town, as represented by their kids, awaited her.

She showered, returned to her room, and pulled on clean clothes, then heard Jacob running his own shower. Despite the storm, they were pretty close to on time.

"Yay us," Addie murmured, "I'm so excited we get to go to school again."

She strolled into the kitchen and got out bowls of cereal for Jacob and herself. A moment later their father wandered into the kitchen, still unshaven, and still wearing that bewildered look that Addie privately thought would be her own expression just as a truck ran her over. He had completely fallen apart when his wife had left, to the point of taking an extended leave from teaching at Dalhousie University.

"Are you getting a school lunch today?" he asked.

"No, Dad. I'll do PB and J," Addie answered. "Like every day."

"Ah, and Jacob?"

"No matter how nasty it is, he'll get the school lunch...same as he does every day," Addie said. "I think he likes the way the lunch ladies make the other kids carry his tray to their table. Jacob wins all the prizes for subtle."

"Yes..." Her father smiled slightly. "He does know how to get along. Shall I make you a sandwich, Adara?" he asked.

He stared at the loaf of bread Addie had taken from the cupboard as if it was some strange mythological beast.

She hesitated. "Sure dad." Her father might be a world-class expert on Celtic and Norse mythology, but he made lousy sandwiches. She pushed the bread and jars toward him. "It would be great if you didn't forget the peanut butter today."

Her father raised his eyebrows and half-smiled. "I'm working on my sandwich-making skill set." He stared at the ingredients until Addie put a knife down in front of him.

"Ah," he murmured. "The missing piece of the puzzle."

TWO

THIS WON'T END WELL
JACOB

Like every school day, Jacob waited at the foot of their driveway for the handicapped bus, his sister standing beside him. Last night had been crazy and grueling, but Addie crackled with new energy. With an inward sigh of weariness, Jacob tried to straighten himself just a little more.

Ever since they had come to this town, something terrifying was changing his sister, and so he didn't dare give into exhaustion. But crazy as the nights were, during the day, Addie stuck close to him – just as she always had.

"You d..don't have to go with me," he told her once again.

"Yeah, like being on the regular bus would be such a good time."

Jacob shrugged. "You could make a f..few friends."

"Why would I need friends?" Addie demanded. "I don't need anyone at that school."

In spite of himself, Jacob grinned at his twin. "No Addie...but a few k..kids there might need you. P..people besides me. Margo and Ryan St. G..george don't con..confine their bullying to us."

"You're psycho," she told him.

He just smiled and looked down the road. "It's here."

The bus pulled up, the door opened, and as he climbed the steps, Jacob returned the driver's daily greeting. As usual, Addie ignored the woman, keeping all her attention on ensuring her brother made it up the steps and settled in his usual place without mishap. Leaning back in the uncomfortable seat, bracing himself against the irregular bumps and jolts of the vehicle, Jacob wondered what new problem would overtake them today. He'd always thought he was pretty good at deflecting the other kids' emotions about his handicaps, but the Port St. George High School crowd weren't like the students at their old school.

On their very first day, he and Addie had run afoul of local mean girl Margo St. George and her bully brother, Ryan. Jacob had experienced their smoldering brutality a few hours in, while clumsily trying to look after his personal needs. Laughing and jeering, Ryan had forced him out of the boys' bathroom and into the girls', then stood mocking sentinel in the doorway.

Jacob had stood in the center of the girls' bathroom, unable to fight back, flushed and humiliated. As always, the radar between him and Addie kicked in, and his twin had arrived in seconds. Giving Ryan a hard shove, Addie pushed into the bathroom to stand beside her brother.

"You okay?" she'd demanded.

He had barely had time to nod before Margo and her friends crowded in. The mean girl sauntered through the door and stood, hands on her hips, while the other girls giggled and sneered behind her.

"I'm Margo." Her freckled face was widened by square bangs that hung down below her eyebrows.

"Congratulations," Addie snapped. She stepped in front of her brother and waited.

Despite his own seething anger, Jacob wanted to tell his twin to shut up, to keep things easy and quiet.

Too late.

Guessing what would come next, Jacob stepped back to brace himself against the wall tiles. No adults would come to their rescue in here. He rested the tip of one crutch only lightly on the cement floor. He might not be able to fight, but maybe he could tilt the coming confrontation in Addie's favor by thrusting the crutch between the bully's legs. It might not help though. Margo looked strong and agile, and chances were the five girls ringing her wouldn't go for a fair fight.

With lighting speed, Margo's hand shot out, slamming Addie painfully in the shoulder. Rubbing it lightly, Jacob's twin returned the girl's hard stare.

"My family founded Port St. George more than two hundred years ago, and we're in charge of everything here." Margo's eyes narrowed. "Neither of you is making a good impression."

"Sorry." Addie stood, hands on hips, and looked Margo over. Jacob's skin prickled like tiny lightning bolts were jabbing him. Addie shifted her weight onto one leg, looking unconcerned, ready to propel herself forward.

"You *will* be sorry," Margo told her.

"Not scared," his twin retorted.

"There's something that feels wrong about you," Margo said stepping closer. "You'd better leave – while you can." She shoulder-bumped Addie and led her posse back into the hallway. "We'll talk soon," she tossed over her shoulder.

"That was just perfect," Addie muttered.

Jacob nodded, and trying hard to look neither embarrassed nor scared, stumped into the hall.

And from then it got worse. Margo's bullying was rarely physical, but a cascade of taunts relentlessly followed the twins through the classes and hallways. With Margo's social hex, no one would risk being the new kids' friend.

As the miserable days crawled by, through fall and winter, Jacob did what he could to keep his sister's fiery temper from leading them into an all-out war with the St. Georges.

"Sticks and stones," he reminded Addie. "Even Margo and her muscle-head brother mostly stop at beating up a cripple."

Addie had practically growled her frustration. But for his sake, she avoided Margo and ignored that the girl was always watching them. Ryan apparently never noticed he hadn't subjugated the twins and, aside from the occasional insult, was working his way through other victims. Jacob hoped desperately that the bullies' power plays would not escalate from cruel words to cruel actions.

The weeks had crawled by, each depressing day much like the next. They twins had gotten through fall and winter, and now spring was easing into the air.

And here we go for another awesome day at Port St. George High School, Jacob thought wryly as he stared out the bus window. The now familiar landscape of rocky coastline dotted with old houses slid by.

By the time the bus picked up its last passenger and then disgorged them all at the school, it was evident last night's storm had put everyone on edge. Unable to stay calm, Addie strode ahead to their locker. Jacob could feel the zing of tension in the air, the shifted eyes and turned-away bodies as he swung down the hall. He kept up the pleasant smile that was his first line of defense but gripped the handles of his crutches tightly.

He never saw it coming.

Margo slid into the hallway from an empty classroom, and in a smooth movement, wrenched the crutches from his hands.

Jacob would have gone down, but was able to grab the handles of a couple of lockers, keeping himself upright by sheer will and rage. He hung there, panting, wanting to weep and curse at the feebleness of his body. Resting his forehead on the cool metal, he closed his eyes, trying frantically to think, to come up with words or actions that would save him from falling helplessly to the linoleum. Save him from complete humiliation.

Would they kick him as they laughed?

Would he simply die from the thundering rage that consumed him?

"D..duh...d..uh...It's so sad being a retard.. retarded crip...crip...crip...cripple," Margo sneered. She poked his shoulder. He clung to the wall for his life. A few girls smiled nervously and the inevitable circle of watchers began to form.

As though it were his own, Jacob felt the rage surge up in Addie's veins. In one quick leap she was on Margo, slamming the girl as she yanked back Jacob's crutches. Kevin Newsom took them and passed them back to Jacob.

"Thanks, Kev," Jacob managed. He steadied himself, lifting one crutch, ready to do what he could to help his sister.

But she had already turned on Margo, fists raised, ready to pulverize their enemy. Margo's face twisted into a jeering snarl but she took an involuntary step back against the lockers. The other kids in the hall circled the three of them silently, waiting for the storm to break across the school; a few looked anxiously over their shoulders for teachers or Cartwright, the new principal.

Breathing hard, Jacob stared at his enemy's face. Margo deserved everything that Addie could do to her...but his twin would be expelled for fighting. In raw terror, Jacob realized that he could not survive in this school without his sister. That their family could not take any more trouble. Pushing down his own anger and humiliation, Jacob stumped his crutches a little closer.

"L..leave it, Addie," he urged. "I..I'm fine and she's n..not worth getting thrown out f..for."

Addie scowled, breathing hard, but with a shrug, began to lower her fists.

"Yeah, Addie," Margo stepped forward and kicked Jacob's crutch. "He isn't worth it."

Like lightning, Addie grabbed Jacob, steadied him, and then drew back and smashed Margo against the lockers. The bully cursed viciously, but then she smiled slightly and raised her fists. A ripple of excitement wavered through the watching students. Addie raised her own fists again.

"Addie, d..don't," Jacob begged.

His sister waited a moment and then stepped back. "Lay off my brother, you witch," she snarled.

"*Principal's coming!*" someone hissed. The crowd melted away.

Margo lowered her arms and strode arrogantly toward a classroom. Her posse trailed behind her.

Jacob and Addie moved slowly toward their lockers. The storm in Jacob's veins pounded, making his head ache and his breath come too fast.

"Th..this won't end well," he muttered.

"You know she had it coming," his twin snapped. "There's something about her and her brother that makes the hair on my neck stand up. They're like…evil."

Jacob frowned. "I d..don't like them m..much myself," he admitted. "But if we get ex..pelled, we'll have to bus it to Bridgewater. Too f..far."

Addie sighed and nodded. "Being around her makes me feel like I've got fire in my blood. Like I want to tear her apart. It's crazy. I've never felt like this before…not even when Mom left." She spun the lock, opened the locker, and began stuffing books into her pack.

"Wh..what are you d..doing?"

"Loading up in case I get suspended."

Jacob leaned against the lockers. "You know I d..don't care when Margo and th.. those kids t..tease me."

"I care. They're evil and nasty and someone should punish them." Addie let out a long breath and met Jacob's eyes. "I can't stand it," she said. "I want to tear her face off...."

He nodded. "B..but you can't. Keep your energy for a f..fight you can win."

His sister slumped. "I don't want Dad to have to deal with me being suspended when Margo reports me."

"She won't," Jacob said. "I'll h..handle it. Principal Cartwright isn't a f..fan of harassment. If Margo reports you, she'll get sus..pended too." He smiled grimly. "I'll r..remind her."

He swung away down the hall trying to decide how to threaten Margo without bringing further reprisals on their heads. Trying not to think about how incredibly stupid it was for their father to have ever brought them to Port St. George. Trying to keep his cool when all his instincts were on fire.

THREE

NOT SCARED

MARGO

"Can you believe that witch?" Karla giggled as they rushed into French class. "And her *buh...buh...buh...*brother. What losers!"

Margo just grunted and slid into her seat. Behind her, she could hear the buzz as her followers relived the fight, took their cheap thrills, and giggled over their leader's actions.

As Madame Smith wrote the assignment on the board and the rest of the class whispered and pulled out their homework, Margo flexed her fingers, uncomfortably aware of the heat flushing her skin and muscles. What was wrong with her?

She could just hear her crazy Uncle Daniel's fierce words. "You're a St. George," he'd endlessly exhorted her. "You and Ryan are the last warrior knights protecting us from the filthy worms." He always nodded his head for emphasis and slapped his crippled legs as a reminder. "Them dragons infested Europe. But we killed 'em. All that's left is the last nest hidden somewheres around here. They killed your father, Margo, and they broke my back, but we ain't beat yet."

His obsession had colored every minute of her life. At his insistence, she'd read the family records, trained herself to be strong and dangerous, imagined that she would be a hero like her ancestors, and tried to ignore their falling-apart lives.

She had almost managed it...but then the Medways had moved into to her town.

The twin's very existence turned her into something she didn't want to think about. Not a hero at all. Maybe just ordinary. Maybe just small. She had tormented a crippled kid. Risked getting thrown out of school. Her skin prickled with the certainty that somehow Jacob and his sister were going to ruin her life.

Simmering, she gazed around at the kids who surrounded her, the ones she had known all her life. Since the day the twins had first walked...make that *limped*...into the school, Margo had felt a jab of wrongness about them, as though sandpaper had been scrubbed over her skin. Whenever they were around, that weird sensation never left her, never relaxed its demand that she stay on high alert. Never stopped whispering that the brother and sister were a sleeping danger.

She hated their family in a way she had never hated anyone before. They had bought the house on the bluff that had once belonged to her own family. That witch, Addie, talked way too much about the cool things she had done while they lived in Halifax, things that Margo had never even gotten close to. And Jacob...Margo gripped her pencil until it snapped under her strong fingers...the cripple who had everything made easy for him.

Not like Sibby.

"*Comment ça va?*" Madame Smith's voice rose as she repeated her question.

Reluctantly, Margo raised her eyes to the board and rapped out the required answers.

Fingering the broken halves of her pencil, Margo promised herself that she would make the Medways very sorry they had ever invaded her life.

* * *

Margo spotted Jacob leaning against the wall when she came out of the girl's bathroom at the start of the lunch period.

"L..let's talk, M..margo," he said.

"Are you sure you c..c..c..can?" she mimicked. Once again her roiling hatred overcame her shame at these cheap shots.

Other than a slight flush on his cheeks, Jacob didn't react to her words at all. Margo looked up and down the halls. Empty. Everyone had hurried off to lunch, leaving the corridors deserted.

Margo clenched her fist menacingly. "You want a do-over?" she demanded.

"N..no," Jacob replied.

He was stuttering a little more – maybe he was scared of her after all. But he stood stoically, leaning on his crutches. Reluctantly, she felt a small curl of respect for him.

"What then?"

"I..if we f..fight," he forced out. "I..if you get the p..principal in..involved, we'll all be sus..pended. M..maybe expelled."

"Duh," she snarled. "I think I know the rules in my own school."

"W..wasn't sure," Jacob replied. He met her eyes evenly. The small curl of respect Margo had felt grew larger.

"No one's around," she murmured. "It could get very painful for you."

To her surprise, the boy's face creased into a tiny smile. "T..to quote my s..sister, *Not scared.*"

Margo laughed suddenly. "You should be, stupid," she said. "I'm watching you. And I'm waiting." With a rude gesture, she turned and headed down the hall to the cafeteria. Rubbery pizza was on offer, but even as she found a seat at an empty table and bit into the slice, Margo couldn't get her meeting with Jacob out of her mind.

Letting out an exasperated sigh, she realized that she wasn't sure exactly what she was watching and waiting for. But the words had crystallized in her mind – those twins evoked a feeling of something scary, something evil.

Something...*dragonish.* The word sprang unbidden into her mind.

Across the cafeteria, Addie Medway was watching. The girl slowly waved a closed fist. Margo opened her mouth to yell a threat, then snapped it shut again. Not the right time yet.

But she would be watching. She would be waiting.

* * *

When school was finally over, instead of heading home, Margo jogged down the road toward Scrace's Marina and Boat Repair.

The marina barely deserved the name. Ted Scrace's ancient dock had slips for about eight boats in a sheltered inlet where the shore eased into a rocky beach. After last night's storm, the dock had been crammed, but only two boats bobbed on the waves this afternoon. Margo barely glanced at the sign proclaiming that gas and the tiny store's few supplies worked on the honor system. She knew Ted would be in the weathered building where, like his father before him, he built and repaired small boats.

Sure enough, when Margo stepped into the workshop, the pungent scent of varnish filled her nostrils. Ted was bent over, carefully brushing a coat of sealant over the upturned hull of a small sailboat.

He glanced her way when she picked up a brush and began working on the opposite side.

"No ninja warrior workout today?" he asked.

She shook her head. "Thought I'd help out here. See how this beauty is coming."

"We can sail her in another week or two," Ted told her. "I think she'll be my best so far."

"Can't wait," Margo replied. With deep pleasure, she surveyed the elegant little sailboat she had helped build. In exchange for her work over the past three years, Ted had taught her some of his inherited knowledge about building and sailing these small craft. The long hours spent were completely worth it to her. On the water, Margo felt free – felt the heavy dregs of her family legacy drift away.

After a couple of hours, they both straightened and Ted grunted his thanks for her help. Margo grinned her pleasure at the work well-done.

She hung out in Ted's shop for another hour, sharing a microwaved lasagna for dinner. It wasn't great, but after her day at school, Margo didn't think she could stand a meal listening to Ryan brag, her mom complain, or her uncle rave. Only her sister, Sibby, would remain quiet.

With a fierce ache, Margo wished she could find a key to open the eleven-year-old's mind.

Afterwards, Margo jogged through the soft dusk along the gravel road that led to the Medway's house a couple of miles farther along the coast. She should have gone home, but Margo felt as though a thin, burning wire drew her inexorably towards the twins. Maybe it wouldn't hurt to keep an eye on them.

A hundred yards from her destination, Margo slowed to a walk. All the lights in the old house on the bluff were on. Apparently the Medways didn't have to worry about the electric bill. With her mom always nagging them, the St. George family lived in chilly half darkness. One of the many reasons she hated going home.

Keeping to the shadows, Margo paced the perimeter of the overgrown yard, watching all the time for movement through the house's small windows.

There they were. Addie walked restlessly around the living room. Jacob leaned over a table, light from a computer screen flickering across his face – probably doing homework. She ought to go home and finish hers, Margo thought. She intended to be the smartest as well as the toughest kid at school.

But at least for now, she would keep watch.

A moment later, Addie strode out of the house. Margo leaned back into the shadow of a wind-tortured spruce, then as Addie headed toward the bluff, Margo followed curiously. What was the witch up to? Her own skin prickled as though lightning zapped the air.

Addie walked back and forth along the edge of the drop, her eyes always turned to the ocean.

"Out for a w..walk, Margo?" Jacob's voice pierced through Margo's absorption. Her breath quickened and the sense of jabbing electricity heightened.

She twisted to fully face him, rapidly gathering her thoughts. "How did I miss hearing you?" she asked. "You being so clumsy and all."

Jacob just stared, but Addie had seen her now and ran swiftly to her brother's side.

"What are you doing here?" she demanded. "It's private property."

Margo's eyes strayed over the house and headland. "My family used to own this," she said.

"Yeah, I know," Addie snapped. "And everything else. But you don't now, so crawl back to your own dump." Her eyes glinted silver in the dark air.

Margo took a step forward but Jacob slid between them. "G..go home, Margo," he said evenly. "Addie and I n..need to work on our presentations for s..school."

Margo couldn't trust herself to speak. Too many bad emotions churned through her, preventing her from thinking clearly. It was like Uncle Daniel's crazy stories were roaring through her brain.

"Eat crab shells," she tossed over her shoulder as she headed back towards the road. As Margo jogged home, she vowed she would get Addie and Jacob for sure – but it wasn't the right time...yet.

FOUR

NORMAL

ADDIE

The spring storms that had been rolling inland for the last few days seemed to have sheered off, but Addie still felt like lightning crawled over and under her skin. She even ran her hands over fabric and touched something metal, expecting electricity to leap into the air.

Nothing.

In a late-night conference held in her bedroom, she and Jacob agreed to never mention a word to their father about the St. Georges' relentless harassment, or even Margo's stalking them at their house. Addie was less convinced about keeping quiet about it at school.

"The principal should know what that witch is doing," Addie argued. "You know the St. Georges bully everyone. It would be a public service to get them thrown out."

"N..not worth it," Jacob countered. "We d..don't know if their friends would k..keep on b..bothering us."

"Ryan, her beastly brother, would love any reason to beat us up," Addie admitted. She sighed. "And I suppose if they aren't in school Ryan or Margo could make all kinds of problems around here. *Keep your enemies closer....*"

She didn't dare tell even her brother that the mounting weirdness in her mind almost had her overwhelmed. Having a bully targeting her too, seemed like one problem more than she could bear.

And besides, every time she was around Margo, it seemed like Addie's own terrifying madness crept closer, hunted for chinks in her thoughts.

Uneasy about Margo's loitering outside her home, Addie took a long while to fall asleep. And then, all night she'd tossed, half-tangled in her sheets, sure that someone called her. That a whole crowd of people called her. Angry voices, loving voices...strange and wild. Demanding.

Demanding what?

When she thought she heard her mom's voice Addie struggled awake, tears running down her face, bereft...angry...determined that no one, not even Jacob, would know about the crazy nightmares. The ones that made her feel like she'd been slit open and dragged out of her own skin.

"Not crazy...just bad dreams..." she told herself grimly while she dressed for school. "And probably it's all witchy Margo's fault."

The reassuring sound of Jacob stumping around in his room, followed by her father's inept attempts in the kitchen drew her almost back to normal.

Why couldn't she feel normal?

But she pretended. At breakfast. On the bus. Walking beside her brother in the school's hallways. She kept her head high, knowing that the covert glances and whispers were all about her and Jacob. About how she had faced down the ruling mean girl.

"Like I need this," Addie muttered under her breath as she stowed her jacket in her locker. When lunch time finally rolled around, she settled at an empty table, slowly chewing and swallowing her peanut butter and jam sandwich. Jacob was smiling and making nice with the lunch ladies.

Out of the corner of her eye, she saw Margo choose her lunch, surrounded by her usual gang of giggly sheep.

Addie huffed her frustration. Somehow she had to get her family back to Halifax, back to some kind of normal life. She just couldn't take these waves of crazy constantly rolling through her mind, getting stronger and fiercer. It felt like the ocean storms had left bits of thunder and lightning inside her.

And then there was Margo churning it up all the time. After yesterday's fight, when Addie had waved a closed fist at her, the mean girl's mouth had opened and closed like an angry puffer fish.

Good times.

With a laugh at the memory, Addie tossed her sandwich wrapper in the trash and headed to PE. She was looking forward to running off some of the crackling energy fizzing in her blood.

Once the bell rang and everyone had changed into their gym clothes, the coach gave his usual lengthy exhortation that no one listened to. Then, with much grumbling and jibing, the pack of boys and girls set out on the required run.

The rush of wind and the distant wash of waves beckoned Addie. Faster and faster she ran, blood pounding in her veins, heart leaping practically into the sky with the joy of movement and power. Within moments, she'd left the rest of the class behind and sprinted up the trail overlooking the ocean and winding behind a thick stand of firs.

The magical, beckoning voices rose in the background of her thoughts and gained power as she breathed in the salty air. They called to her, and in the mad dash, Addie forgot her fear of them, rejoicing in the words she could almost hear.

The rollicking wind and slapping waves urged her on and on. She held out her arms and felt as if she could leap into the air and soar over the ocean.

Power.

Freedom.

And then, a pitiful cry. "*No! Leave me alone!*"

With an almost physical crash, Addie felt herself snap back into herself. With intense irritation, she rounded a bend in the path and came upon the eleventh-grade bully boys. Ryan St. George had his forearm against Tyler Jenn's chest, pinning him against the rough bark of a spruce tree. He and two of his buddies were yanking up Tyler's gym shorts in a series of hard, painful wedgies. Tyler flailed his thin arms, hands clenched into weak fists, and even from fifteen feet, Addie could see the moisture on his cheeks.

Ryan St. George jerked around when she paused. "Move on, witch," he snarled.

"Up yours," Addie tossed out. Tyler was nothing to her and she'd had enough trouble with the St. Georges. And worse, the beautiful freedom of the voices, the rush of power she'd felt, had dissipated like morning mist.

"*Stop...please...*" the victim panted, clutching ineffectively at Ryan's muscled arm.

Chafed by the empty feel in the air, Addie shrugged. Tyler was just another loser. He needed to learn to fight back. Like she'd had to.

Like Jacob couldn't.

"Oh crap on a popsicle stick," she muttered. Turning around, she stalked back to the three boys tormenting Tyler. "You're done now. Let him go," she ordered.

For a moment, surprise stopped the boys. Then Ryan faced her slowly, rotating his shoulders to display his muscles.

"I'm going to give you to the count of three to disappear," Ryan sneered. "One...two... *thr...*"

Addie balled her hand into a fist and slammed it into his nose. Ryan yowled his surprise and clapped a hand to his face. As his blood flowed, Addie's rose again to fever pitch.

Lightning, thunder and wind howled through her heart and mind.

"*Run...!*" she roared.

Silver mist filled her brain; wind shrieked around her. Addie screamed her rage.

They ran. It was the last thing she saw before the ground spun, silver clouds consumed her, and she passed out.

FIVE

SAPPHIRE
JACOB

Bored to screaming, Jacob stared out the art room window.

"Great job," the art teacher intoned as he paused for the obligatory positive reinforcement.

Lousy job, Jacob mentally corrected.

"Thanks." He wasn't even half-trying to draw the still life, because despite his physical therapist's insistence that sketching would improve his fine muscle coordination, Jacob just didn't care.

But his life had enough pitfalls without adding a teacher's dislike to the mix – especially when a smile was so easy. Besides, he thought, surveying his lumpish classmates, working at this school must be a miserable job. The teachers needed all the encouragement they could get. His mouth quirked in genuine amusement, but his eyes strayed back to the window.

Addie and the rest of his class were at PE, running track. For only an instant he allowed himself to wonder what it would be like to simply race along, feeling wind on his face.... Speed! What would it be like to fly along the track under the power of limbs that weren't weak and awkward? Well, unless someone came up with a medical miracle, he would never know. Distastefully he picked up his pencil again.

But a flash of movement by the woods caught his attention. Four boys were tearing down the path, not in a runner's measured lope, but pelting and stumbling in terror.

And then, above the trees, a flash of silver, so brilliant it hurt the eyes.

No, no! Not now! Jacob dropped his pencil and grabbed his crutches. Trying to keep the noncommittal smile on his face, he stumped to the wall where the bathroom pass hung. He shook his head at the aide-du-jour and, moving as fast as his unwieldy body would allow, headed down the corridor to the outside doorway.

He knew that flash. Only he knew what it meant. Day and night he had been watching for it, dreading it. The wildness born into Addie's blood had woken up. Just like their mother had warned him it would.

"No, no, no!" he pleaded to the air. "Not here. Not now...please..."

Staggering down the steps, he nearly fell. His breath came hard, his feet caught on the uneven gravel, but he kept thrusting the crutches forward, swinging his body in the pendulum rhythm he was condemned to.

Forward. Back. Forward.

Faster.

He had to go faster.

He had to get to his sister before it was too late.

And all the while, over his labored breathing, above the shaking exhaustion in his arms, he replayed the last conversation he'd had with their mom before she had finally disappeared.

"I know she's like me," his mom had said. "She has the wildness in her blood, and sooner or later, her blood will win." She looked scornfully around at their suburban house. "You have to look after her when it happens, Jacob. When the change comes on her."

"B..but what about you?" Jacob had demanded. "Won't you l..look after her?"

She looked at him beseechingly. "I...I'm sorry. I just can't hold it off any longer. I'm burning up inside......I've tried so hard..." Her fingers fumbled to push back his sleeve and expose the silver bracelet on his wrist, a thick cuff worked with carved runes. "Try to convince Addie to wear hers...they'll help." She touched his cheek. "I'm so sorry, Jacob...."

She was gone by morning.

He thrust the memory away. Thrust his anger away. No good thinking about it.

Had to get to Addie...

Almost, he was almost into the trees. Jacob's breath knifed in his side, but he kept going. The wind carried the voices of the coach, the shriller shouts of the trailing kids half a field away. Pretty soon the teacher would head this way, then the students would follow behind...maybe the principal...maybe paramedics.

If they saw...if they guessed, everything would be over. And what would happen to Addie then?

Jacob looked back over his shoulder and swore. The teacher and kids were coming. He had to reach Addie. He had to protect her from herself.

The swaying trees cast uneven shadows across the ground. And the form that had been Addie, cast a larger one. Jacob caught his breath. He had known, but he still was unprepared for the sight before him. The dragon lay on the path ahead as though asleep; wide silvery wings spread around her.

"*Addie!*" Jacob's cry wasn't much more than a croak.

Addie lifted her great silver head, eyes the color of an ocean storm, taking him in. She raised her head even higher as the sound of pursuit floated on the wind.

Jacob stumped closer to her. Sunlight shimmered like liquid across her silver skin.

"Change b..back," Jacob pleaded. "Change back, Addie. Before it's t..too late!"

Even as he watched, her storm grey eyes gleamed defiance and a smile clearly played across the silver lips.

"Addie, p..please! For me!"

The nightmare had awakened. Jacob couldn't stop the tears, the fear of what would happen.

"Jacob," she hissed. Then her eyes appeared to roll back into her head and she collapsed. A glitter of silver mist surrounded her, and then his sister lay unmoving on the ground.

Jacob staggered over, casting aside his crutches as he fell down beside her. He held her hand and tried to stroke her face. Her eyes opened again, her own grey eyes that were so familiar.

"Hey, bro," she whispered. "What...what happened?"

"You c..collapsed."

"No, I didn't...couldn't..." She frowned, puzzled.

"Just take it easy," Jacob said. "No b..big deal. I'll look after every..thing."

Addie's eyes drifted almost shut, but then he felt her muscles tighten and she looked up at him again. "No worries. I got this."

When the others reached them, Addie leaned back against her brother, white-faced, eyes closed. But Jacob could see the determined twist of her mouth.

The coach knelt down by Addie, felt her pulse. "Call 911," he ordered one of the boys. Ryan, his buddies and victim hovered behind them.

Jacob thought fast. "H...heat," he stammered. "Addie over..heated."

"But she hit me," Ryan shouted. Blood had dried on his face and stained his shirt.

Jacob felt unaccustomed passion erupting within him. If he weren't a cripple, he would pound them all. But his body would never do that. His fighting had to be done with his brain. Determined, Jacob struggled silently to keep control, to keep his mind fast and clear.

Addie needed him.

"No," he said firmly, his glare holding Ryan's eyes. "It was the g..guy out here in the w..woods. Using drugs...and...and he had some fireworks too. You guys startled him. Addie t..told me...then she fainted."

Ryan looked uncertainly from Jacob to the coach. His face hardened as his gaze fell on Tyler's tear-streaked face.

Ryan turned on his victim abruptly. "That's right, isn't it, Tyler?" He dropped his arm over the other boy's shoulder, gripping painfully. His voice held the promise of vengeance.

Tyler's fists balled and then abruptly his shoulders drooped. "Yeah," he said slowly. "A big guy. Creepy."

Addie's eyes were wide open now, and Jacob could see the control returning to her as she sat up. "Big, creepy guy," she repeated to the coach. "Scared the crap out of me."

"Language," the teacher muttered. "Take it easy. Don't move too fast."

"I'm okay now." Addie's gaze lingered on the bullies and a little smile played around her mouth. "I was just scared, especially when Ryan and his friends ran off and left me."

Ryan scowled under the coach's look of contempt, but Jacob held in a laugh. He could relax. Addie was back in charge...for the moment.

The security guy rolled up in a golf cart; the coach supported Addie into the passenger seat, and then they whisked her off to the nurse's office with the kids from the PE class following behind like a pathetic parade. Jacob waved off the offers of concern and help. He had to think, and the slow return to the school would give him time for that. At a distance, he spotted his aide standing by the door poking at her phone. Jacob veered toward the most distant entrance. He had to ditch that woman.

He needed to figure out how to save his sister. Needed to finally understand the curse his family existed under.

Four. He had been only four when he wakened from sleep and wanted his mom. No one came when he called, so he'd flopped out of bed and crawled from his room along the dark hallway. He still remembered the exhausted shaking in his legs, how they'd given out, so he had dragged himself on his arms, feverishly determined...determined...and then out the window he'd seen....

The end of class bell rang. Jacob stopped and leaned into a shadowy alcove in the brick wall. He'd holed up here before – a sanctuary where he could stay hidden from his aide and the students streaming to their next class. Shudders ran through his body. Pain from weak muscles that had been pushed too hard sliced through his hips and shoulders. He'd just wait. The pain would pass as it always did. He would not give in to his body's weakness...he would keep his spirit strong...a strong spirit and an agile mind lasted longer than a strong body.

And then he snapped. Jacob threw his crutches across the pavement, listened to their hateful clatter. He was panting, trying and failing to thrust away his frustration and fear. His legs gave out and he slid down the wall; tears he couldn't hold back ran down his face.

Helpless. Useless. A body that barely worked, but *he* had to protect his sister. Why had their mom given up and left? Why was their dad so...so oblivious to everything?

Jacob wrapped his fingers around the bracelet he wore under his long sleeve.

"It holds symbols for inner peace and finding your way home," his mom had said. "I put all the magic I could into it...."

Jacob tried to bring his thoughts, his breathing...*himself,* back to his own control.

Student voices clouded the air and faded as the kids rushed to their next period.

He wondered if his aide had noticed he was AWOL yet. No one had any idea how much he longed for peace. Right now, he desperately wanted to leave this stupid school and go home.

The bell signaling the start of the next class shrilled, startling a pair of crows into flight above the school, both squawking their harsh displeasure.

Jacob watched the birds' slow circles against the glass-blue sky, tried to hear the distant wash of waves on the shore, let his breathing slowly calm. His hand dropped from the bracelet and his mind drifted.

He was in the sky circling with the crows, looking down in careless indifference at the school below. His strength felt endless and he was free....

"Jacob...*Jacob!*" The aide's strident voice penetrated his brain. His dream self spiraled back down into his broken body. His eyes flew open to the schoolyard's hot pavement and the face of the aide leaning over him.

"What?" He couldn't summon his ready smile – he had been powerful and free, and then this ghastly woman had snatched him back.

"Are you okay, Jacob?" She thrust her face even closer to his, so that he was forced to breathe in the flowery perfume she wore. Angrily he pushed her back, shoving her face away from his.

"Leave me alone!"

Calm, he told himself. *Anger gets you nothing...be calm.* But the anger felt like a snarling beast inside him.

"I'm okay!" he managed. "Dropped my crutches." He pointed to where the things lay on the pavement. He took another deep breath. Now he forced the smile, hoping it wasn't too thin, too fake. "I took some time for a quick nap, before you looked for me."

The aide's eyes narrowed at the implied insult, but she got the crutches and helped Jacob to his feet. Once he was upright, she didn't let go of his elbow. For a moment, Jacob just stood, seething that her hand was on him without permission. Wanting to swing a crutch into her, wanting to lash out. They stood, not moving for what seemed a long, long time.

"Jacob!"

Jacob's chin shot up. "Dad? What are you doing here?"

The aide finally let go and stepped back as Jim Medway strode toward them. "The school called me about Addie, but no one seemed to know where you were."

"He just took off…" the aide complained.

"He outran you on crutches?" Jim's eyebrows raised in disbelief. The aide flushed and without another word stomped off in the direction of the office.

"What a dreadful woman. Are you alright, Jacob?" His dad touched his shoulder gently.

Jacob met his eyes, and before he could stop himself, he leaned forward onto his father's chest and felt the strong arms encircle him. Muffled by the cotton of his dad's shirt, Jacob allowed all the fear and rage to escape in silent sobs that shook his entire body.

Neither spoke until he was still, and then all his dad said was, "Want to walk or should I bring the truck around?"

"Truck," Jacob said. "Kind of a l..lot of excitement today."

As his father hurried toward the parking lot, Jacob got his easy smile firmly back in place. Straitening his shoulders, he experienced a small surge of triumph. His mind was his own again and he had mostly kept it strong. Leaning against the wall, waiting, Jacob turned his thoughts back to his sister. And to the St. Georges who tormented them both. Addie was right – there was something innately evil about them. But if Addie took them on, no matter how much they deserved it, she might reveal the secret she didn't even know she had.

Jacob had to outsmart his twin. Somehow, he had to save her from herself. He just didn't know how.

SIX

DRAGON SLAYER

MARGO

Margo threw her backpack onto the dilapidated ladder-back chair in the hallway. Ryan obviously wasn't home yet as the hallway hadn't been littered with his gym clothes, sports gear, jacket and backpack. In their living-room-turned-hair-salon, she could hear her mother happily telling a customer about her childhood in Alaska.

Margo was hungry and still angry at the way the week was playing out – she couldn't forget that that spaz Jacob had let her know she'd get in big trouble if she tried to report his sister. And they thought *she* was a witch! Margo's skin practically burned with the sensation that something weird surrounded those twins. But what? And how was she going to carry on the family legacy of protecting the town from evil? Especially when she had no idea how to recognize it when she saw it.

Or if it was even real.

Bitterly, Margo thought she might pound on everyone like her brother did – that way she'd be sure to get someone who deserved it.

She hesitated by the kitchen, but caught the gossip between her mom and one of the town's old bags. "Newcomers, those Jenns," her mom's customer was saying. "And they think they're something special because they bought one of those new houses on the ridge."

"You know what that woman said to me?" Margo's mom demanded.

Before she had to listen yet again to her mother's bitterness over the latest insult – every day there was a new one – Margo turned abruptly and made her way to the back porch where Uncle Daniel was sure to be. At the sound of the screen door closing, he lowered his binoculars and twisted around in his wheelchair to face her.

"No activity today," he reported, as though there ever had been anything new. He gestured to Margo's younger half-sister, Sibby, working at the chipped picnic table with reams of paper and chalk pastels. "But our seer sees another storm on the horizon."

As usual Sibby did not look up or acknowledge her sister's presence. As usual, Margo gently touched her shoulder, but the eleven-year-old only twitched a bit.

"Any sightings at all?" The question was half ritual, half request, almost mocking.

Her uncle frowned and pointed toward the ocean. "Nothing specific, but I got a feeling they're moving. And Sibby's drawings are showing storms and specks off in the distance. Except for one." Daniel turned his wheelchair to face the table and sifted through the pile of Sibby's drawings. "This one is real different."

He held up a picture of a thick stand of woods with the ocean framed behind it. In the center of the path, a grey cloud obscured the trees.

"What do you make of this one, Margo?"

With a sense that her heart had skipped beating for an instant, Margo recognized the trail behind the school. She didn't think Sibby had ever been there. Her sister was terrified of leaving the house, and after the school refused the family's petition for special classes four years ago, after Sibby's dad had left, their mom gave up. She'd even kept all her kids home for a year in protest. Bonus as far as Margo was concerned – it had given her time to build the training yard beside the house and hone her combat skills. But finally, the school went to court to force Margo and Ryan back to classes. Nothing was done for Sibby, so their mom left her youngest daughter to draw all day beside her crippled uncle.

"Hey, what's this?" Margo pointed to the drawing.

Sibby raised her eyes. "They're here," she said.

"Who are here?" Margo wanted to shake her sister free from the locked world of her mind. And she'd like to pound her uncle too, who spent his days watching for the dragons he said had killed Margo's father and broken his own back. She was convinced his terrifying stories had further handicapped the unwieldy workings of Sibby's mind.

"The dragons," Sibby said. She bent her head back to the drawing she was working on – a cave-slashed coastline where icy waves hurled against cliffs. Blue, green, and white specks swirled high above.

Her uncle leaned over and gripped Margo's arm. "You hear that?" he demanded. "The time is coming again – and it's going to be the St. Georges that save the people!"

Heat rose in her face, and Margo wasn't sure whether it was the old surge of pride that the St. Georges were the dragon slayers, or anger that her uncle lived only for this insane obsession.

"Sure," she said, "I'll get right on it."

He let go of her arm and scowled. "Don't forget that a dragon killed your father." He gestured down at his own useless legs. "And did this to me. We're the last knights in the Crusade, and we St. Georges don't forget our duty. Father to son, for twelve centuries."

"You might have noticed, I'm a daughter," Margo snarled.

Her uncle continued as though he hadn't even heard her. "We got nearly all the dragons in Europe. Out there," he gestured toward the sea, "that's the last nest of worms. If she hadn't broke my back..." His mouth twisted like was chewing something horribly bitter. "...your father and me would've sailed up the coast until we found them. Hiding out in sea caves somewhere. We would've killed them all. We built the boat ourselves. Perfect little craft..." He turned to Margo, eyes eager and glistening again. "But you've been training. You and Ryan are nearly ready." He gripped her arm again. "The boat's hid real close. Pretty soon Ryan'll be ready – he can take it and go there. Finish it. Finish them."

With a sense of revulsion, Margo yanked her arm back and rubbed the bruised skin. Her uncle simply settled back into his chair and stared out at the slate grey waves stretching into the empty horizon.

Sibby looked out at the water too, but then her eyes drifted back to her paper. She picked up another grey-colored chalk.

Feeling like she might throw up, Margo turned on her heel and went up to the tiny bedroom she shared with her sister. Climbing to the top bunk, she searched under her pillow for the chocolate bar she'd stashed. Its sweetness melting in her mouth only slightly eased the bitterness in her mind.

She wanted to pound the wall. Her family was like a cats-cradle of rubber bands pulling her in too many directions. Sometime soon she would snap. If she could be like her brother Ryan, just mean and mindless, it would be easier. How did Uncle Daniel imagine that Ryan could ever do anything that needed planning?

She took another bite of candy, then impatiently rewrapped it and shoved it back under her pillow. Mean and mindless was the best way to go. The St. Georges had founded this town, according to her uncle and the old diaries, in order to hunt down the last dragons. The family records claimed a few sorry remnants of the mythical beasts had traveled here with the Vikings centuries ago.

They supposedly nested in hidden caves along the wild coastline.

But who had really seen a dragon? Was her whole family crazy? Was it some big delusion that they'd carried on, generation after generation? It went round and round in Margo's mind until her head ached like one of those fantastical creatures had clawed her scalp. Look where this obsession had gotten the St. George family – not heroes, not respected, not anything. Just dirt poor with nothing to show for two hundred years of so-called duty, nothing except a shabby house, a car that didn't run, and worn-out pride in a half-deserted town.

Margo's lip curled. There were so many reasons to hate the Medways, all sad because their mom was gone and Daddy quit his job. They didn't know what tough was. Margo's dad was dead, dead three months before she'd been born, carried off by a collapsing bluff during a gale while he and his obsessed brother hunted something they imagined was a dragon. Margo was pretty sure the whole town laughed behind their backs while oozing pity at the family's crazy ways.

No one was going to pity her – that's why she made sure she ruled the high school. Yeah, she'd really like to pound them all.

They St. Georges had been rich once. But now, all the money her family had was her uncle's and sister's disability pensions and the few dollars her mom could make cutting people's hair. But that spaz, Jacob Medway, got to go to school in a special bus, while Sibby was turned away because the old principal said that none of the teachers knew how to teach her. All he'd offered was to send her off on the two hour bus ride to Bridgewater – Sibby, who couldn't leave the house any more because she was so afraid of the dragons Uncle Daniel wouldn't shut up about.

Margo pulled a pillow over her face to muffle her curses of frustration. Then she hugged it to her chest and bitterly tried to figure out a way to get the Medway twins, once and for all. She was pretty sure getting them kicked out of school would make her feel a whole lot better.

Anything that didn't have to do with dragons would make her feel better.

SEVEN

STORMS AND SECRETS

ADDIE

Riding home in the truck, squished between her dad and brother, Addie couldn't decide whether she was more sleepy or more hungry. Or more confused.

She knew something weird had happened. But she couldn't remember anything clearly after that burst of righteous anger when she'd had it with Ryan and Margo and the St. George gang of bullies. It was as if all her bad feelings had gathered into a wind-whipped storm and then howled through her brain and blood. A hurricane with a streak of silver shooting through it. A nightmare she didn't want to think about. What would have happened if Jacob hadn't been there? A shudder ran through her body.

"You okay?" her twin asked.

Addie nodded. "Tired...and really hungry. If we still lived in Halifax, Dad, we could go to a drive-through for a burger." Thinking about a big greasy burger and salty fries made her mouth water.

"I'll barbeque tonight," her dad told her with the kind of smile that was supposed to be loving and warm, but looked more like a grimace on him these days.

"Fine." What difference did it make anyway? It wasn't like a burger could solve their lives. But if there was a milkshake too....

The truck growled its way up the bluff road, bouncing over the stones that had worked up through the gravel during the winter freezes and thaws. The nearby crash of waves almost drowned out the rattle and roar of the vehicle.

Nothing can defeat nature, Addie thought suddenly. And this town was all about nature. The houses, even though they were scary-old, perched like sea birds on the rocky land. The people here stuck with their timeworn ways as determinedly and inevitably as the seasons turned. As though any kind of change would turn everything to dust.

Addie shivered. What if they had to somehow defeat this whole town?

"We should move away from here," she said suddenly.

Her dad looked at her as though he didn't understand the words.

"I know this is where you met Mom," she went on desperately, "but we know she won't come back here to find us. She'd look for us in Halifax."

Her dad pulled up in front of the house and switched off the engine. "I know you dislike Port St. George," he said. "I do too. But there's a reason we have to be here. Your mom would have wanted it."

"Would have wanted us to live in a town where everybody hates us?" Addie demanded furiously. "That makes no sense."

"We d..don't get this," Jacob said more evenly. "If there's some kind of…secret…about why we're h..here, don't you think we should know, Dad?"

Their father shook his head. "Nothing you need to worry about."

Addie saw her twin's face whiten and a tight look crept around his mouth. Angry, she saw with shock. Jacob was really angry.

"This is crazy!" Addie shouted. "What's the big secret?"

Both her father and Jacob stared out the windshield, both breathing hard. Jacob's hands were clenched.

"So don't tell me," she snarled. "Why should I care that my whole life is crap and you won't tell me why!" Flinging open the truck door, she scrambled over her brother, jumped out and ran across the property toward the sea.

She could breathe by the ocean. She had to breathe.

In the rush of wind off the water, she forgot about her hunger, forgot about everything except the need to feel cold gusts on her face, smell salt-laden air, and hear the roar of waves as they crashed over the slick rocks that ringed the narrow beach. Abandoning her brother and father, she raced through the straggly woods to the headland where she could look out over the ocean, look for miles across steel grey water.

Above, the gulls sang a chorus of discordant shrieks and squawks, skimming over water, floating on waves, picking and quarreling over some delicacy washed ashore. The surge had receded, exposing the barnacle-crusted rocks gleaming with seaweed, jeweled with tidal life. Sandpipers strutted and pecked among the stones.

There was an easy path down to the narrow beach but Addie couldn't wait. Instead she flung herself down the bluff, ignoring the scrapes and bruises, wild to get to the shore, to the wind and water, to...

"Addie!" Jacob's shout brought her back from the brink of...what? Where had her mind and heart been going?

The shock of the thought left Addie panting, weak-limbed. She sank down onto a driftwood log, elbows on her knees, needing to clear her head, needing to remember not the wild dreams, but herself – Adara Medway, daughter of Jim and Audra Medway. Fifteen. Student at Port St. George High School. Mother AWOL. Father a grieving mess. Brother…brother who needed her….

Addie lifted her head and forced herself back to her feet. Jacob was slowly making his way down the path, and even though she felt like her own limbs were as heavy as sodden sailcloth, Addie walked over casually, like she had just wandered over to be with him. Ready to catch him if the crutches stuck in sand or slipped on rock.

"Great day," she said gesturing to the heart-breakingly blue sky and the glittering roll of waves beyond the rocks.

"Addie, you h..have talk to me," Jacob said. "What is h..happening?"

"Talk? I thought I was talking?" Addie sparred for time. Jacob simply stared at her, waiting. There was nothing she could hide from her brother and he would be relentless. A trickle of anger and resentment ran through her.

Addie picked up a smooth stone and sent it skipping through the foam on the crested waves. The anger swirled in her again. Did it ever stop now?

With a shock, she realized that ever since their mom had left, the anger had been there, beneath her skin, like a long, slow snarl. The beast in her didn't want to be held down any more, didn't want to lie sleeping under a good-girl act.

Not that her act was so good.

"I think I'm going insane," Addie said at last, her voice so low she knew Jacob would have to strain to hear it. "Nightmares...all the time. Now they're crawling into the sunlight... and at school..."

She turned suddenly to her brother. "Jacob, what if I lose it, really lose it and hurt someone? I'm feeling so strong, and the nightmares just make me feel stronger. What if I do hurt someone?" she repeated desperately. "I want to, Jacob. Margo and Ryan St. George make me want to hurt them."

Jacob looked back at her, blue eyes darkening. Then he turned his head and stared out at the ocean, as though scanning for a ship.

"This is the part where you tell me I'm imagining things." Addie gave his arm a poke.

"Y..you're imagining things," he said obediently and laughed, but Addie could see the smile didn't reach his eyes. He glanced down at her bare arms as though suddenly seeing them. "Where's y..your bracelet?" he demanded. "The one M..mom gave you."

Addie scowled. "In a drawer somewhere."

Jacob held up his arm and shook back his sleeve. The bracelet glinted on his thin wrist. "Isn't it a t..twin thing?" Once again, the joke didn't reach his eyes.

"No, it isn't a twin thing," Addie snapped. "It's a mom thing and I don't want to wear one of Mom's bracelets. She's done with us. I'm done with her. And who cares anyway?"

Jacob sighed, sank down onto one of the logs, and carefully propped his crutches within easy reach. Addie sat down beside him.

"Remember M..mom said the bracelets have a symb..bol for inner peace," Jacob explained. "Maybe you could u..use it?" Once again Jacob made it sound like a joke, but Addie knew it wasn't.

"I told you, I don't want it," his sister snapped. "And I guess jewelry is a lot more important than the fact I am completely going crazy!" She couldn't believe he wasn't listening to her.

Jacob clasped his hands on his knees, staring down at the sand.

"Don't you have something to say that will make me feel better?" Addie prodded. "I'm not joking about feeling insane."

"I kn..know," he said. And then nothing. He just stared at the sand.

"So, what do you think?" Addie demanded. She wanted to shove him, make him answer her, give her something to help fend off the nightmares that were crowding into her mind. But he stayed silent.

Didn't he get it?

"In my head, it's like there's a storm coming," she said finally, struggling to explain the wildness of her feelings. "Like when we sit at the top of the bluff. First the sky off in the distance gets crowded with grey and black clouds, like they're fighting each other as they tumble our way. Then the water gets still and quiet, like the waves are gathering strength before they attack the shore. The birds fly inland, away from what's coming. The wind begins to blow..." Addie's voice rose, taking on a sing-song quality. "First steady, then gusts that bend the trees over and snap them back. And all the while the storm is rolling closer and closer...."

She put her head down in her hands, trying not to cry, trying not to be stupid.

"Where is the st..storm now?" Jacob asked. He gripped her hand and squeezed.

"I think the winds are gusting," Addie whispered. "I think the storm is rolling in and it will carry me away. Soon."

"I won't l..let it," Jacob said, his voice hard. "I'm your anchor, Addie."

She leaned her shoulder against his and the two of them stared out at the silver-grey ocean until their father called them to come in for dinner.

EIGHT

NIGHTMARES

JACOB

Jacob left his family in the kitchen and headed upstairs to his bedroom as soon as he had swallowed half a burger. His sister was hungry all the time these days, and so he'd lured her back into the house with talk of the grilled burgers and waiting slabs of cake. The tension of all this was making him incredibly hungry as well – but even more exhausted. He'd been yawning his head off while he ate, because while Addie paced the shore, roiling with fear that she was going insane, Jacob watched, knowing it was worse.

Much worse.

Stumping awkwardly along the hallway, he thought he could sleep for a week. But all he had was maybe three hours before his sister finally gave up and decided to go to bed. He had almost reached his own room when he suddenly remembered the bracelet.

Maybe he couldn't make Addie wear it during the day, but if he slipped it on her wrist at night, perhaps they both might get some sleep for a change. His mom had said it was magic; his mom knew magic...and Jacob was desperate for any help he could get.

Once in Addie's room, he looked around in despair. His sister was a dedicated slob. Clean and dirty clothing lay in heaps that only she could decipher. Her desk was stacked to teetering with books, ancient DVDs, and a mish-mash of craft projects she hadn't touched in months.

"In a d..drawer somewhere," Jacob muttered. He nearly crashed when one of his crutches became wound in a pair of jeans tossed on the floor. Swearing softly, he allowed himself to tilt over and grab the dresser for support. Carefully he pulled out drawer after drawer, searching for the bracelet. Nothing, except more evidence that his sister wasn't just a mess in her head.

Exasperated, he yawned and leaned on the furniture. Her nightstand had a drawer. And naturally between him and that drawer lay an obstacle course of the detritus of Addie's life. Scowling, Jacob grabbed his crutches again and tried to weave between the piles.

He stumbled once when his crutch got caught in a discarded gym shoe, but he crashed onto the bed where the untidy heap of blankets, sweatshirts, and a duvet saved him from all but irritation.

Rolling over, Jacob pulled open the drawer and fished through the tangle of ear buds, tissues, hair brushes, and miscellaneous items that Addie had stuffed inside.

"I don't know how you even close it," he muttered. He had a sudden vision of the old illustrations of dragons sleeping on a hoard of gold and gems. Dragon Addie would probably nest in a pile of old clothes, scrunchies, books, and computer cords.

The smile on his face widened to a grin when his fingers slid over the contours of the bracelet. He could feel the silver's engraved triple spiral edged with deep blue lapis lazuli. It had been the night of their twelfth birthday that his mom had explained that the bracelets were incredibly old, that the symbols held the elements of life together to create inner strength and peace.

"And they will hold you together," she had said, pressing one on his bony wrist and offering the second to Addie, "if the passions in your DNA start to overwhelm you."

"Like wh..when we become teenagers, all crazy hor..mones," Jacob had joked.

As his fingers caressed the familiar symbol, he remembered that Addie had grimaced and twisted the bracelet loosely in her hands. Their mom had responded to his joke with a sad smile.

"Something like that," she'd murmured. She gripped his arm. "Promise me you'll never take it off, not even for a moment," she insisted.

"This is dumb," Addie had muttered.

"Jacob?" His mom had looked at him in desperate appeal.

"Okay...."

"Promise," she repeated.

"Okay, I p..promise!" He had said it like a stupid joke but his mom had looked so desolate. Maybe because of that he had never had taken it off. Not when he slept, not in the shower. Never.

Jacob closed his fingers around his twin's bracelet, untangled it from some broken wires, then shoved it in his pocket. Stifling a yawn, he pulled himself up from the bed and managed to make his way out of the room without tripping.

In his own room, he set the alarm on his phone and without getting undressed, collapsed onto the bed. He was asleep in seconds.

He was in the middle of that soaring dream again when the alarm began to beep at him. Forced awake, Jacob lay for a moment staring at the dark ceiling, trying to recapture the sense of freedom, of being able to move without stumbling, of having great muscles that flexed and obeyed his mind.

Knowing he had to get moving, Jacob muzzily forced himself to his feet. He hadn't heard his sister or father go to bed – he'd been too sound asleep, but the house was dark. The thud of his crutches would not awaken anyone – they were too used to his awkward noises as he moved around his room or went to the bathroom. Despite that, he took as much care as he could to set the tips down without a thump and to avoid lurching or stumbling.

"Keep it e..ven and slow," Jacob told himself softly. It gave him some control – not much, but some.

He crossed into his sister's room without mishap. She hadn't touched the piles on the floor nor heaped anything else on the chair, but she was curled into a tight ball under her blankets, breathing evenly. Jacob sat down and glanced at the clock. Midnight.

He had to stay awake somehow for yet another vigil.

But he was so tired.

A flash of anger shot through him. Maybe he should just let it happen. He didn't know how long he could prevent Addie's DNA from surging through her, transforming her once and for all into a dragon.

She was her mother's daughter, Jacob thought. A wild creature who couldn't live in a house and go to school...or be her brother's only real friend.

Jacob blinked hard and leaned back. How long would it be this time before the nightmares would claim his sister?

Too soon.

Within minutes, she began muttering in her sleep, first a mumbled word here and there, then quiet groans. Jacob sat up in the chair, eyes never leaving her form. She tossed fretfully and the blankets slid to the floor. Addie's arms lifted as though reaching for something, dropped again, then reached up, fingers clawing the air.

She was panting and Jacob's heart lurched as he saw the silver sheen begin to quiver across her skin.

"N..no," he whispered. "Oh, Ad..die!"

He remembered then, and, mentally cursing his own exhausted stupidity, yanked the bracelet from his pocket and heaved toward his twin. She was thrashing now, moaning as though something hurt a lot. Desperately he grabbed for one of her arms, but she jerked away from him. New strength filled her body. The silver sheen grew into a halo of light.

Silently, Jacob grappled with his sister, finally seizing and holding one groping arm with both of his. Were her fingernails turning silver? How far had the change gone already?

Tears streaming down his face, he threw his entire torso over her arm, pinning it down against the mattress. Desperately Jacob forced the bracelet over her wrist and flipped the clasp. Then he lay there, panting, holding down her arm, scanning her face, looking desperately for signs that his twin was still there.

Her eyes flew open. Silver. Slitted. The eyes of a dragon. Blinking in fierce intelligence. But then the color faded and Addie's own grey eyes looked back at him blearily.

"Jacob?" she muttered. "I had the weirdest dream..."

Her eyes fluttered shut. The silver glow around her died down, quiet darkness filled the room, and her breathing settled into that of deep sleep.

Jacob slid off the bed onto the floor. For a long while he buried his head in his arms, forcing back the sobs.

He had won.

Tonight.

The wild magic would not claim his sister tonight.

In complete weariness, Jacob crawled to his abandoned crutches and hoisted himself up on the chair. Somehow, he managed to make it from there to his own bed without falling. Once again, not bothering to undress, he pitched forward into the welcoming softness.

As he slipped into sleep, the question rose into his mind...how long? How long before he lost Addie to the wildness in her blood? And what would he do when that happened? Somehow, Jacob had to save them both.

But how?

NINE

SILVER
ADDIE

Early morning sun washed through the bedroom window as Addie opened her eyes slowly, still caught in the dizzy feeling of being between dreams and waking. Lifting her arms to stretch, sunlight glinted off the silver bracelet on her arm.

How did that get there?

Then her eyes riveted on her fingernails. Silver. They had definitely turned silver during the night. The soaring dreams, the howling through her veins, the weirdness she'd felt ever since they came to this town...and now this.

What was happening to her?

Heart pounding, she held up her hands again, letting the sunlight shimmer on the living silver. Her breath came faster and faster. The dream of leaping into the air, screaming her determination, spiraling down through the icy fog to...where? It had seemed so real.

Her fingernails had turned silver.

Puberty, especially when it hadn't arrived until she was nearly fifteen, was supposed to be tough. But this? The sex-ed classes had promised a lot of bodily changes, but never this one. Not once had silvery fingernails been mentioned.

Addie sat up, pulling her knees to her chin and wrapping her arms around her legs – hugging herself, hiding the fingernails from her own gaze. But the movement caused light to reflect off the silver on her wrist again. The bracelet. The one her mom had given her. Somehow, during the night's weird dreams she must have reached out for it and slipped it on. Unexpectedly, her eyes filled with tears, but she angrily wiped them away. She didn't do crying. Not ever.

"So, yay...I'm turning into some kind of freak," she muttered. "Like my freaky family living in this freaky town isn't enough. Now, I've got weird, mutated DNA. Thanks, Mom."

Addie let her memories stray over their growing up years. When other mothers sipped coffee with friends or went to work or cleaned up the house, their mom had played with them, or sang to them, or told them amazing stories. She made everything seem like magic.

But Audra Medway didn't work, or car pool, or whip up cookies for the bake sales. When pestered into participation by the other moms, she'd practically created pyrotechnics at PTA meetings.

"At least I'm used to being a social outcast," Addie consoled herself. She held up her fingernails again, reluctantly loving the slivers of light they sent dancing over the walls of her bedroom.

Gorgeous. Freaky. But gorgeous.

Bitterly, Addie guessed her friends, if she'd ever had any, would envy the silver sheen she'd probably inherited from her mother. But they didn't know the cost of having Audra Medway for a mother. Nothing normal about their childhood – no soccer games, no vacations to theme parks, no birthday parties. Only their mother's crazy. Every weekend and holiday, Audra had hauled the whole family on near-survival hikes along the Atlantic coast. Even Jacob.

Smart people sheltered from the gales along that rugged shore. With tears streaming down her cheeks, Audra ran from the car and staggered into the salted wind, calling and begging the invisible somethings that haunted her thoughts.

Addie remembered too clearly how the years had played out. Their father followed

Audra's every urging – he would refuse her nothing. But when Addie and Jacob got old enough to rebel at camping in the bitter oceanside winters, their mom had frantically paced the house and finally left them with their dad and gone anyway. How many hours had their mother wasted staring at the ocean at Port St. George?

"I met your father there," she had told the kids. "It's near my family. And...and it draws me back."

"Why?" Addie had demanded.

"Because Port St. George is the place where I found my chance to have you," their mother had said sadly. "But there are too many against us. They made me give up a part of myself."

Scowling, Addie slowly twisted the bracelet on her wrist, debating whether to toss it in the drawer again or wear it to school. The cuff's intricate silver etching and semi-precious stones would make Margo burn with envy. Hating Margo kept Addie from thinking about what was happening to her.

"I won't be like everyone else," Addie declared rebelliously.

Especially here.

Grimly, she curled her fingers into silver-tipped claws. She'd give practically anything to leave this town, but the St. Georges would never get the satisfaction of making her run. This bizarre change to her fingers would incite Margo to...what? The witch would circle in and make Jacob her first target. Addie scowled. Giving up her pretty new nails to protect Jacob didn't even compare.

Silently, she slid out of bed. Camouflage would be needed. When Addie saw her toes gleamed silver too, she wiggled them regretfully. She could handle this.

Avoiding the creaks in the warped floor, Addie eased down the hall past her brother's and father's bedrooms. In the bathroom, she chose the least noticeable tint left from her mother's wild selection of nail polish.

Black wouldn't have been her own first pick – silver was *much* prettier – but some of the girls used dark colors.

And why did her fashion-oblivious mother always wear nail polish? While painting her finger and toenails, Addie tried to remember if she had ever seen her mom's nails without a coat of lacquer. Resentfully, she decided that this fantastic change in her body had to be a straight up inheritance from her strange mother.

Why had her mom never told her?

Didn't moms have to do the mother-daughter thing? Like, "Let me tell you about the birds and the bees and creepy fingernails?"

Blowing on her nails, dully black now, Addie heard an alarm go off, followed a moment later by the thud of Jacob getting out of bed.

"Time for school," Addie muttered. "Life is just so good."

* * *

"Pencils down."

Addie put a last flourish on her seriously unflattering cartoon of Margo and laid down her pencil, smiling angelically at the teacher. She had calculated exactly how many questions she had to answer to earn a passing grade, completed them, and with twenty-five minutes to go, spent her time far more amusingly on the portrait.

Ms. Neville picked up Addie's paper between two fingers like there was dog dirt on it. "This was a test," she said.

"Yes, ma'am," Addie said brightly, "and you'll find I earned a strong C."

"You could have had an A," the teacher said sorrowfully.

Addie grimaced. "What good would an A do me?"

The teacher shook her head and moved

on. Addie let only a touch of a mocking smile creep across her face, then looked over at Jacob, still laboring away, while his aide stared out the window in profound boredom. Jacob's brain worked so much faster than his hands that Addie had no idea why he was not always simmering with frustration. She would be yelling and throwing things, fighting her way through every day.

And it wouldn't do a bit of good. Jacob knew that, had known that since his first days in pre-school. So he used smiles to fight his way through the world.

"You are clearly my hero," Addie said softly. The bell rang. She picked up her backpack and headed out to PE, hoping that running another mile or two might help.

But remembering what had happened during the last gym class, Addie hesitated. Instead of joining the throng of kids jostling their way to the change room, she trotted out of the building and veered toward the stand of trees that hid the trail. Her memories of the previous day were vague, like a nightmare that held chills and then was gone. But there had been something wonderful in that memory too, and she wanted it.

She heard a shout behind her, but ignored it. She was so over this school. A few seconds later, the lacework of shade closed above her. Sounds from the school faded and the swash of waves against the nearby shore rose up and muted everything else. Addie stood among the trees, swaying a little with the rhythmic echoes. Slowly she paced along the path; when the tangle of brush got in her way, she left the trail to get to the water. Determinedly she beat down snarls of vegetation and clambered over stacks of driftwood until she reached the stony beach. With a long sigh of relief, Addie stood with her toes at the very edge of the lapping water.

The sea called her, powerful, loving. Her breath deepened as her lungs and blood filled with the salt and scent. Addie raised her arms, tilted her head back to feel the sun on her face, became barely aware of the thrumming in her blood.

And then...*Thwump!*

Addie staggered into the water, caught her balance, and whipped around. Margo St. George stood behind her, laughing, ready to shove her again.

Enraged, Addie paused for a moment. Then in fury, she dove at her enemy.

The two girls grappled, trying to trip each other, grunting and swaying, fingers clawing into the skin of their opponent. Margo grabbed

Addie's hair and yanked viciously. Addie kicked, toe connecting with Margo's knee.

Their fight was silent. Too serious for taunts or threats. The only sounds were their shoes scuffling on the stones, the splashing water, and their gasping breath.

Addie fought desperately. Margo was bigger, much stronger, and clearly used to fighting. An instant of panic flickered in Addie's mind. They were alone out here. What would Margo do to her?

Harder.

She had to fight harder.

Where was the roaring strength that had consumed her the day before?

Margo's fingers dug into her shoulder and Addie could have screamed in pain. She pulled her knee up, trying to butt her enemy in the stomach. Margo was too fast. Instead she grabbed Addie's leg and wrenched it around. Addie howled in sudden pain, completely lost her balance, hanging half in the air while Margo yanked up her knee.

Then it was over.

With a contemptuous heave, Margo threw her into the lapping ocean. Addie went down, her injured leg as awkward as a broken wing. She choked as icy water filled her mouth and shocked her system.

Margo stood on the shore and laughed.

Somehow Addie got to one knee, rocks and barnacles digging painfully into her skin, waves pushing her this way and that. She knelt, head hanging, knowing she would have to crawl over more sharp, slippery rocks to get to shore. Unsure if Margo would beat her more, would throw her back into the water until she drowned.

She looked up. The laughter had gone from Margo's face and the bitterness of her expression was as much a shock to Addie as the salty water.

Addie was shaking now, pain and cold sending shudders through her body.

Margo sloshed forward into the knee-deep water and held out her hand to Addie. "You and your family better leave this town," she said.

She waited impatiently, hand outstretched. "I beat you," she mocked. "I don't have to keep beating you."

"So you aren't going to kill me?"

Margo's face twisted. "I'm only trained to kill one thing. Get out of the water. I don't want to be expelled."

"Really?" The tide was slipping in and she wasn't going to get out of the waves any other way, so Addie reached for the girl's hand.

As their fingers touched, a zap of power flashed over her. Like Margo was connected to an electric current.

Margo yanked back her hand and Addie fell again into the water.

"What?" Margo demanded. "What did you do, you witch?"

"Me?" Addie hissed. "What did you do?"

Rage bubbled on Margo's face. Her fists clenched. Addie prepared herself for another beating, but then the other girl gave a snarl of rage, spun on her heel, and took off, back toward the school.

Trying not to cry in pain, Addie crawled from the water. The rising tide seemed to help her, the waves lifting her a little over the sharpest of rocks. On shore, she flopped back onto a small patch of sand, ignoring the hard bumps of wave-smoothed rocks under her back.

The pain in her knee made her gasp. But not cry. Addie didn't cry. She could endure. She lay in the cool sun for a long time, until she heard the distant bell echoing over the playing field, mingling unnaturally with the swash of water. The tide crept closer. Addie shut her eyes and wondered if it would be a pleasure to let the ocean carry her away into its depths.

But that would leave Jacob alone.

Fighting back the agony, Addie rolled over and scuttled and crawled the short distance to the heap of driftwood. She heaved herself up to a sitting position on a log and poked through the tangled debris until she found a sturdy branch. Once she'd shaken off the clinging seaweed and broken off jutting twigs, Addie used it to push herself up onto her good leg.

Leaning on her makeshift crutch, she hobbled back up to the trail and toward the school. She'd never felt so helpless.

How can Jacob stand feeling so weak? she wondered. *And how am I going to make Margo pay?* Addie smiled fiercely, letting her plans for revenge dull the pain in her leg.

Margo's going to pay!

TEN

THEY'VE FOUND US

MARGO

Margo made sure no one noticed her return to the school. Taking a detour to the girls' bathroom, gave her a minute to think.

What had happened when she offered her hand to Addie? Margo looked at her own fingers wonderingly. She'd never felt anything like that before. Had that zap of whatever been there when she and Addie fought? She didn't remember it. But she'd been so elated by the chance to take out her rage on the witch, she might not have noticed.

It had shaken her a little to see how ferociously her enemy had fought back. Margo was used to the girls she'd grown up with – they cried and whimpered and slapped their hands a little. No one, not even the rough and tumble boys, had ever fought so hard, so fiercely. Addie had no trained moves, but she sure gave back as hard as she could.

Margo felt a slight stirring of respect.

"That's okay," she told her battered reflection in the mirror. "It's okay to respect your enemies."

She wondered uneasily what would happen now. Maybe she'd gone too far, yanking Addie's knee like that. But she'd been so angry for so long – and the witch deserved it – strutting around the school like she was some kind of queen.

Was she the kind of queen to go to the principal and get her enemy thrown out? Principal Cartwright had made it really clear that a fight like theirs meant expulsion, not a slap on the wrist suspension. Margo considered if getting kicked out would clear the way for her to accompany Sibby to school in Bridgewater. Stupid idea. Sibby wouldn't go – would be a wreck long before the bus made it that far.

And anyway, Margo wasn't about to be pushed out of her own school.

She spent a few minutes drying her hair and clothes, then swaggered out into the hall when the next bell rang. Let the PE teacher mark her absent. If anyone dared ask, she'd say it was that time of the month and she was looking after things. A smile flickered over her lips. She'd used the excuse twice in the last three weeks, but it wasn't like anyone would actually check.

In the Myths and Legends class, Addie was – surprise! – absent. But when that spaz, Jacob, stared at her for a long time, Margo felt a twinge of apprehension. Those twins were so weird who knew what they might do.

She really hated them.

"...And, as I explained last week, we'll begin our presentations on legends tomorrow," Ms. Hamilton was saying. "I expect at least two sources for your information. Even though I do encourage you to research the mythology of your family's ethnic background, only one source can be from a family tradition..."

Margo met Jacob's eyes challengingly. The kid smiled too much, but he wasn't smiling now. With a slight shock, Margo realized that the expression in his eyes was the same fierce determination she'd seen in his sister's face.

Uneasily, Margo wondered again if maybe she had gone too far. She was supposed to be a dragon slayer...or a teenage girl...or the last of the Port St. George town founders...or who knew what.

None of those meant beating up someone just because she didn't like them.

None of them meant being mean and mindless. That was her brother's gig – and her brother was a moron.

Margo rotated her shoulders uncomfortably. Too bad. She was who she was...and her family or the town or her uncle's stupid dragon-slayer obsession weren't going to decide who she was or what she was supposed to do. She'd decide that for herself.

"Questions?" the teacher asked.

Bitterly, Margo realized she didn't have anything but questions. And none of the answers she'd come up with were making her feel any better.

It was a relief when the bell finally rang.

* * *

Ryan's gear and his idiot friend's stuff were all over the front hallway. Margo looked in disgust at the mess. Aside from the heaps of their smelly gym clothes, a half eaten sandwich had fallen out of Sean's bag and dribbled mayonnaise and wilted lettuce onto the floor. Ryan's nearly empty notebook lay open with a muddy footprint on the blank page. She could hear the boys in the kitchen shouting and crashing around, so instead of heading for the fridge and the snack she was longing for, she turned toward the porch.

Uncle Daniel had left a cigarette burning unheeded in the ashtray and a mug of coffee parked on the table. Sibby was dropping crumbs on today's drawings as she munched some store-bought cookies. Margo pulled one out of the open bag and bit into it distastefully – cheap and stale. This evening, she'd make some oatmeal cookies. Sibby liked them and the kid got even less than Margo did to make her happy.

Margo touched her sister's shoulder and pushed back her own disappointment when Sibby shrugged away under her fingers. Not today. Her sister was deeply absorbed in her drawing. Unreachable.

"So how was school?" Uncle Daniel asked flatly, his eyes straying out toward the horizon.

"Okay," Margo answered. She slid onto the bench beside Sibby, but faced her uncle. "I have to do a presentation tomorrow for my Myths and Legends class. Thought I'd do it on how St. George killed the dragon."

"It's not a myth," Uncle Daniel snapped.

Margo again pushed back her irritation. "The teacher and everyone else in the universe think it is."

"They're too blind to see the truth," Uncle Daniel retorted. "We St. Georges have kept the people safe for centuries. They've forgotten."

"Right." Margo pulled a notebook from her backpack. "So let me remind them. Tell me the story again."

Uncle Daniel's mouth worked like he was chewing something bitter. Margo waited with her pen ready, trying not to be impatient.

"So back more than a thousand years ago, more like 1400 years, there were a lot of dragons all over the world," Uncle Daniel finally began. "I was told there were all kinds, mostly bad, but the ones in the British Isles were the worst. This one dragon nested in the middle of a bog – all water and sucking mud – right on the edge of a settlement. And every few days it would fly into town and pick up a cow or a sheep to feed on. All the cattle were being killed and even though the people threw stones and shot arrows at it, the dragon never minded. And there was this sickness too. People said it was the dragon's foul breath...."

From the corner of her eye, Margo saw Sibby start on a new drawing. A swamp was taking shape under her chalks, with a lone girl tied to a tree.

"...so the king decided to trick the dragon by feeding it the people who were already sick."

"What?" Margo demanded. "Could he do that?"

"He was the king," Uncle Daniel said scornfully. "He could do anything he wanted."

"Terrific king..."

"You listening or not?"

"I'm listening. It's just gross," Margo retorted.

"You're too soft." Uncle Daniel spat over the railing into the weeds. "You don't get how bad the world is because of dragons. Everyone would've starved because of the stolen sheep, and the sick people would probably have died anyway."

"Great," Margo muttered.

Uncle Daniel glared but continued. "So, anyway. Now the king's daughter gets sick, so the people tell the king she's next. So she's up and tied to the tree, crying, waiting for the dragon to eat her. And along comes Sir George, a knight. He sees what's happening, unties her, and when the dragon comes, he fights the beast and kills it." Uncle Daniel's face shone in bitter triumph. "That was the first. He took the princess away – she didn't want to stay there anyway – and started hunting down all the dragons he could find. And the princess and St. George's kids, and their kids, and so on, all the way down the St. George line have done the same. We keep the lands safe; it's our sacred duty...."

"So long as you can walk," Margo snapped. Her uncle jerked around and swung his hand to slap her, but she pulled back. "What has our sacred duty done for us?" She stood, her words tumbling out at a shout. "You're crippled, my father's dead, and we're broke. And wait! There aren't any dragons!"

Margo shoved her fist in her mouth, as if to dam the avalanche of anger. She hadn't meant it. Hadn't meant to lose it like this. Unaccustomed tears filled her eyes and she angrily wiped them with the back of her hand. Trying to get her mind off it, she turned toward Sibby...and froze.

The picture of the princess had been pushed aside.

On a clean sheet, Sibby hurriedly swept the chalks across the paper. The shoreline by the school appeared, the waves, the screaming gulls. Driftwood, trees, sparkles of sunlight on the ocean.

And then a figure was sketched in. Margo recognized herself – fighting, grappling, but not with Addie Medway. Under Sibby's hand, the image that appeared was that of a great silver dragon.

Margo had the dragon by one clawed leg. Its wings beat the air and its great head rolled skyward in pain.

"They've found us," Sibby whispered.

ELEVEN

FIND THE MAGIC
JACOB

Jacob didn't believe a word of the story Addie told that night – that she'd skipped class and gone to run on the beach instead. That a stray stone shifted under her foot and she'd gone down, twisting her knee in the process.

"M..must have been some crazy stuff on that b..beach," he told her. "Your f..face is scratched up, too."

His twin glowered at him and shifted the icepack to another sore spot. Their father had already turned away to pick something out of the freezer for dinner, so he missed the glares his children exchanged.

"Make sure you put some antibiotic ointment on it, Adara," he said over his shoulder. "Pork chops or spaghetti?"

Dinner was another silent meal. Their dad asked the required, "*How was school, today?*"

and probed no further beyond their traditional response of, "*Fine.*"

Jacob's stomach churned at the realization that his sister had been in a vicious fight. And that something even more important had changed – for the first time ever, she refused to confide in him. A glance under his eyelashes showed Addie moodily stirring her pasta around with a fork.

Not so cool and in control after all. Jacob shrugged in annoyance. If she wasn't going to trust him, he wasn't going to push her.

"Dad," Addie spoke up suddenly, "we have to do a presentation about a myth in school tomorrow. I want to do it on St. George and the dragon. You're the mythology expert. Can you fill me in?"

"What?" Jacob felt a shock ripple through his spine. "No...not the St. G..georges. Not d..dragons..."

Addie looked at him coldly. "Margo is doing it on that topic. Ms. Hamilton said up to three kids per legend, maximum. She's one. I'm two. You're three."

"Not a good id..dea," Jacob hissed. "Besides...I w..wanted to do M..medusa."

"Too late." Addie smirked at him. "I've already emailed the teacher. And," she pointed her fork at their father who had left the table and was pulling books down from one of the shelves that lined every room. "Dad's already on to the research. Are you going to tell him to forget about it?"

Jacob glared. He hated it when Addie manipulated him. But the look of dull misery on their father's face had lifted for a moment and Jacob couldn't take that spark of relief away from his dad either. Even if it meant playing into the simmering feud between Addie and Margo St. George. But it really made him mad. This was just asking for trouble, and Addie had never purposefully done that before.

Could the awakening in Addie's blood be making her crazy?

"Popular legend about St. George and the dragon is, of course, no where near the truth," their father said happily as wandered back, flipping through the pages of a large book. "First of all, St. George was from Libya."

"I th..thought he was an English knight who s..saved a princess from a dragon that was g..gobbling up all the people," Jacob objected.

"That's what it says online," Addie added. "I checked it out at school."

"Really?" their father demanded. "Online? Where any fool can write any fanciful trash and muddy real information? *That* is your research, Addie?" The tone of his voice blended horror and sorrow.

"It's a g..good starting point." Jacob smoothed – he didn't want the lecture about reliable sources. Just because his dad was an academic expert didn't mean he or his sister cared. Jacob smothered a laugh when their father rolled his eyes – Addie did it just the same way. Clearly she'd inherited some of her mannerisms from their dad, not just their mother.

Dr. Medway sighed and continued. "The real St. George was a Roman soldier, a Christian, who was eventually beheaded for his beliefs. His story drifted back to England during the Crusades at least 800 years after he died." Their father paused and stared almost unseeing at the far wall. "Do you want the historically verified research version, or the real story?"

"Could you be telling us there's more than one 'true' version?" Addie demanded. Sarcasm dripped in her voice. Jacob jabbed her.

"Yes, there is, Adara. That's why meticulous research is critical."

When she rolled her eyes, their dad's mouth quirked into a shadow of a smile, but then he sat down at the table beside them. Dr. Medway closed the book, straightened it so that it aligned with the table's edge, and then leaned forward.

"The mythology of dragons is incredibly tenacious…every culture…every civilization over the centuries has stories about dragons, from the Pueblo Indian feathered serpent to the Chinese imperial dragon. The persistence of these legends world-wide hooked me into this field of study years ago. What could it mean that the same sorts of tales were repeated all through history?"

"Don't know, Dad," Addie snapped. "Why don't you tell us?"

Dr. Medway didn't seem to notice his daughter's sarcasm. His voice dropped like he was relating an old and dangerous secret. "Dragons have existed alongside humans since the dawn of time. They are fierce, wise, old, and terrifying. In the typical St. George story, the dragon symbolized evil. Dragons are even used in Christian mythology to represent the devil."

"Why?" Jacob demanded.

"Because they can't be controlled or explained," their father said softly. "They are from the time of magic – the time before religion or science ruled us."

"So, St. George wasn't a hero?" Now Addie leaned forward, eyes flashing. "Just a big, bullying fake?"

It was Jacob's turn to roll his eyes. He was getting a really bad feeling about Addie's plan for their presentation.

"What's the r..real story about St. G..george?" he asked, desperately hoping this would steer them back to the topic he cared about – a decent grade and no true dragon information for his sister. The compelling tone of his dad's voice...this insidiously different view of the world, completely terrified him.

What if...? Jacob shook his head as if to clear it of smoke. What if Addie made connections to what was happening to her? No! Their life was complicated enough without the two of them suddenly being part of some old legends.

He gripped his hands under the table. He'd have to deflect this somehow, but he had no way to stop his expert father who was on an academic roll.

"The verified history of St. George began in Libya," their dad went on. "The town lay in the middle of a swamp, and was consequently riddled with disease. The king was a petty tyrant and a complete fool," their father explained. "That much historians agree on. But other sources, not...immediately available, give a clearer picture."

"What sources?" Addie demanded.

"I've pursued different lines of research...." Their father hesitated.

Mom... Panic flooded Jacob. "So wh..what happened to St. G..george?" Jacob probed. *Go with the story...don't talk about where the story came from,* he pleaded silently.

"Yes, well," Dr. Medway said and leaned forward again. "The dragon, Knukor, part of the mid-European clan had been visiting with a northern African clan. On his way back he caught the stench of burning flesh and diverted closer to the towns to look around. He found massive funeral pyres outside a village that flew the plague flag. His sympathy aroused, he tried to enter the town but those who could still stand threw stones and shot a few arrows at him to drive him off – they'd long forgotten that dragons have the power to heal. When the king ordered those wretched townsfolk to 'sacrifice' sick people to him, Knukor took them, one by one, and used his magic to breathe healing into them. Then he carried the victims to a better location. They were happy to get away from the king.

"But the strain of healing and saving so many people weakened him terribly. When St. George showed up, Knukor was close to death himself. His sacrifice had been too much for his strength and magic. St. George dragged him, wounded and suffering, into the town to demand that the people convert to Christianity; then St. George killed Knukor." Their father paused, his hands curling into fists on the table. "St. George's fame made dragon killing an obsession for all his descendants. You can't know the disaster he caused. Dragons were hunted almost to extinction. There are so few left...so few."

Jacob's mind reeled. "So few?" he demanded. "There are...there are more?"

"More, yes." His father looked at him sadly. "They've made so many sacrifices to survive and preserve the old knowledge. But they're dwindling. Without people helping, they will disappear from the world."

Jacob sat back in his chair, mind whirling. He felt like he could hardly breathe. Could hardly fathom what he had heard. His mother had not been some weird, isolated difference. His head felt like it would explode from the realization. How could he not have guessed?

Why hadn't he ever thought it through?

"A..are they here?" His voice quavered more than usual. "M..mom?"

"Of course." Dr. Medway sounded surprised at the question. "I'd been researching ancient Viking settlements along this coast – Vikings revered dragons, you know. I found

Audra hunted, wounded. So beautiful, so magnificent. When she changed into human form, I carried her away and nursed her back to health." He swallowed. "I loved her so much. And she loved me...us..." His voice was husky with grief, but he forced a smile. "But the wildness in her blood is too strong. I keep hoping she'll remember and come back to us. That's why we had to come here – it's where I first found her."

Their father's eyes filled and tears slipped silently down his cheeks. He wiped them with the back of his hand, then got up and began removing their dinner plates as if nothing had just happened.

Jacob turned to his twin. Addie stared at their father's slow-moving figure, her eyes smoldering in fury. Abruptly, she shoved away from the table.

"I'm going back to the internet," she tossed over her shoulder. "At least those crazies are believable."

She doesn't get it, Jacob realized. *With everything that has happened to us, how can she not believe him? Why won't she believe him?*

Then the reality washed over him. Whether Addie believed the story or not, her own wild heritage was stirring. The storms rolling in off the ocean, her rivalry with Margo, all were zapping awake whatever DNA she carried.

Human Addie and Dragon Addie were at war.

How could he keep his sister safe? Safe from herself...and which self was she supposed to be?

Jacob sat at the table, breathing hard, eyes going first to his father methodically cleaning up the kitchen, then to the hallway echoing with furious bangs and crashes from Addie's upstairs bedroom.

Jacob half-laughed. Even though his life was collapsing around his ears, he still had a project due for tomorrow's class. Such was the life of a teen.

Slowly, Jacob pulled the laptop from his school bag and flipped it open. He'd stick to the garbled myths reported on the internet. Addie was right. Even those fanatics' fantastical dragon stories weren't as weird as what their father had just told them. No one...no one at all would believe his own family story.

He had to stay focused...had to stay normal for Addie, for all of them.

Normal.

Jacob paused and stared at the screen, the light flaring against his eyes. But what if it was true...? If there were dragons nearby...? If his mother was one of them...?

Magic. His heart leapt. Dragons and magic lived in the world. He could find the dragons and find the magic. Find his mother. Find some kind of reality to live in beyond his own flashes of memory and his father's crazy stories.

Maybe his half-broken body wouldn't matter. His breathing quickened and he was distantly aware that his hands shook as he went online. If he chose it, a noble quest could lie before him – one that could save his family.

And somehow, maybe, it would save him too.

TWELVE

HERE BE DRAGONS

ADDIE

Addie hurled another book into the heap in the corner of her bedroom, then froze. The fight with Margo had chipped tiny flakes of polish off her nails. Silver gleamed beneath the black lacquer.

She sank down on her bed and wearily rubbed her aching leg. What was happening to her? Spreading her hands, she studied the lustrous silver peaking through the dull polish. The flicker of light caused her blood to surge in joy. Experimentally, she curled her fingers into claws, then sighed. Silver or not, Margo had beaten her soundly today.

"You are such a loser," she declared and flung herself backward onto the bed. Staring at the ceiling she held her hands up and let the shards of light dance across the walls and ceiling. Then bored, she dropped her arms.

For several moments she brooded over the many awfulnesses of Margo, the school, and her life. She longed to be back home in Halifax where she could catch a bus to the mall, or get a burger, or go to a movie, or do any of the things that felt normal. She'd never had a lot of friends, but it hadn't mattered because she'd had Jacob.

So what had changed with her twin? He kept smiling but beneath it was a moodiness that had never been there before. It was like he was keeping secrets from her and worrying over them.

It had to be all Margo's fault, she decided. Addie had been so laser focused on whatever meanness Margo was coming up with, that she'd barely run interference for her twin. And Jacob was way too proud to complain or whine about the fallout of their dad's insane move-to-this-forgotten-town-to-find-their-mother fiasco.

As always, Addie recognized Jacob was braver and stronger than she was.

"What's wrong with me?" she demanded of the air. Once again she watched her silver-tipped fingers reflect light against the walls. Her mouth tightened. More important – what was happening to Jacob and what could she do about it?

Maybe he wasn't coming off as unscathed from the bullies as he pretended. Addie replayed the mental footage of their days at the Port St. George High School. Jacob said it was fine, but she realized now that he'd had none of the easy camaraderie from other years. Sure he was different from other kids, but he'd always had friends. In fact, Addie thought wryly, he was the one that always got invited to birthday parties. Her temper had never made her popular.

"*Bad Addie*," she murmured. She hadn't cared so long as Jacob had friends and belonged. "But neither of us belong here," she said aloud. Her father was pathetic, mooning around as if his wife, Audra, would come looking for them. If her mother loved them, she shouldn't have left.

The memory made an uncomfortable pricking of loss in her mind...Addie refused to go there and sat up, scowling. She didn't care if her mother ever showed up. There wasn't anything to think about except that her father was crazy, her brother was in trouble, and she was determined to beat Margo St. George any way she could. If she could take down the bullies, kids would welcome Jacob like always. Getting to her feet, Addie limped away from her bed, fished around under a pile of clothes for her laptop, and snapped it open. She'd start with outshining Margo on this project.

Pathetic, but right now it was all she had.

* * *

Picked to go first, Jacob stood stolidly before the class, wooden-voiced, stuttering harshly, his presentation projected on a screen behind him. Addie clenched her hands under the desk, feeling sympathy-sweat dripping down her back. Bright pictures, some music, even some embedded footage from a history show flickered on the screen, but Addie knew there was no substance in her twin's work.

Smoke and mirrors, she thought grimly. The teacher didn't seem to notice. She smiled and congratulated him on the technical knowledge that had shone in the project. Ms. Hamilton didn't know that Jacob could do technical with his eyes closed, but he usually worked the content to a crazy high level as well.

Not this time.

"Margo," the teacher said. "You're next."

Margo glared at Jacob as she hauled an unwieldy cardboard mounted display up to the front. Her freckled face flushed as she propped it up. When it tipped over and fell to the ground, she scowled and fumbled the set up. A few kids in the back snickered. Maybe Margo had bullied a few too many people, Addie thought with an inward smirk.

The teacher waited patiently while Margo righted the board and faced the class.

With a shock, Addie saw the board displayed not garish pictures and crooked printing, but historical maps showing migrations, weather maps, and neatly printed annotations beneath them. Margo stared out over the class. The laughing, the whispers, the bored shifting in chairs stopped entirely.

"*Here be dragons*," she said in a low, penetrating voice. "The St. George's have been dragon slayers for centuries; we're the heroes that protected the towns and people from these unnatural reptiles." She surveyed the kids with contempt.

"Do you think you are safe because of modern technology?" she demanded. "Dragons are linked to the first evil, the fall of Adam and Eve. They were behind the Viking scourges in the dark ages. We think they brought the black death to Europe – there were more documented dragon sightings at that time, than ever before or since."

"Margo..." the teacher hesitated. "I've asked you to use verifiable sources."

Margo nodded, her nostrils flared. "I have. 'The Icelandic Sagas' – if you've ever read them – are verified records about how the Vikings explored this coast hundreds of years before Columbus. They brought the dragons here to escape the European hunts. Those hunts were huge – hundreds of dragons were destroyed by my ancestors in central Europe. But the dragons tried to save themselves by flying north. And the Vikings helped them."

Margo turned and jabbed her finger at a carefully hand-drawn map. "These weather maps show prevailing winds across the northern Atlantic and they match up to the accounts of Viking exploration." Her hand swept across the chart. "You can see that the dragon sightings correspond – and move steadily westward."

"But where did you get all this?" Ms. Hamilton's eyes widened in confusion.

"My family have kept records," Margo told her coldly. Addie was sure her lip curled. "Dragon slaying has been my family's destiny for more than a thousand years." She stared directly at Addie. "We don't forget and we can't be fooled."

Silence. The class didn't move at all. Even Ms. Hamilton seemed bewitched into immobility.

"Remember that. We can't be fooled." Margo picked up her display and walked, head erect, back to her seat.

Addie watched, fear and anger growing in equal measure. Her heart thumped with the tangled emotions. The battle on the beach yesterday was clearly only the beginning. Her breathing came harder and harder. The anger was building a fire inside her, one that lit her blood and raced across her mind.

Dragons.

Without waiting for Ms. Hamilton's request, Addie leapt to her feet and strode to the front of the room. She didn't bother to switch the computer screen to her own presentation. It seemed stupid now. Her mind felt like ancient winds were whispering in her thoughts. Her safe, internet-informed presentation was pushed aside in the sure knowledge that unfolded in her thoughts.

How could she have doubted?

"I am going to tell you a story," she said. Her voice throbbed with authority. "Listen to my story.

"More than a thousand years ago, the great dragon Knukor flew over a town where the stench of burning bodies fouled the air. Below him, the town hoisted the plague flag. Ever since the belief in Adam and Eve and the spread of Christianity, dragons have avoided people – they know that they have been branded as agents of the devil.

"In fact, dragons carry the oldest knowledge of creation. And more important, they carry the gift of healing...."

Addie felt the power growing in her, as she retold the story. She glowed with the truth of it...her voice rang with belief.

"Addie..." Ms. Hamilton's voice came weakly to her ears.

Addie ignored it. Power surged through her. She was aglow with conviction, as if a torrent of knowledge poured into her mind.

Distantly she saw Margo get to her feet, eyes wide. Addie lifted her head, felt the power growing in her limbs. Dizzy. Wildly alive. Incredibly ancient...she was part of it all....

"*Oof!*" She grunted.

On the floor. Jacob on top of her, pinning her down.

"*What...?*"

Struggling, Addie fought back the anger, the confusion. What was happening? She felt sick, dizzy. The world seemed to be spinning. In crazy clarity she saw Jacob rip off his bracelet and slam it onto her wrist. Calm seemed to radiate up her arm from the silver against her skin, uniting with the soothing coolness of the bracelet on her other arm.

"Jacob! What are you doing?" Ms. Hamilton shrilled. "*Kevin...call the office!* Margo, sit down!"

Addie stared at the ceiling, aware that the spinning was lessening. Aware that her twin was holding her down, begging her to stop... stop what?

And her enemy, Margo, stood over her, light blazing in her eyes. Lip curling in savage triumph.

Addie struggled weakly for a moment... she had to fight Margo...had to protect Jacob from the witch...had to...

The room spun again. Addie heard herself moan softly as she spiraled down into the dark....

THIRTEEN

HER FATHER'S BOAT

MARGO

Margo flew along the road toward home. The exultation...the certainty...and it was all true! The scourge of dragons was true! And they were here, living in Port St. George.

The father she had never met had died a hero, not a drunken fool! And Uncle Daniel wasn't crazy after all. Relief from long-held shame poured over her and her heart panted with the joy of it.

Even the run-down house and the pathetic stories her family had clung to were proof that the St. Georges mattered. That they had held onto their history...their destiny, for centuries. And she, Margo St. George, had been born into a long line of heroes who protected their people from ancient evil.

Margo's feet slowed in her headlong dash for home. She paused at the top of the small hill and looked down the road at what passed for a business section – the general store with its tiny post office, the garage where Eddy Newsom fixed cars and trucks, the bed and breakfast house that hardly ever had customers, the small church that needed a coat of paint.

Margo sat down on a big stone by the side of the road and stared. The air smelled of salt from the ocean with a tinge of oil from the garage. A few people strolled down the road; a couple of chattering teens left the store carrying cans of pop; Eddy helped push a car into the cavern of his shop. With a sense of blissful belonging, Margo watched them.

Her town. Her people.

She was destined to be their hero. To save them. With a laugh, she wondered if they had any notion of how closely the town teetered on the brink of ancient magic...ancient evil. Margo flexed her arm, relishing her hard muscles. She was strong and ready.

Then she got up and, head held high, strode toward home.

In the front hall, she slung her backpack onto the floor and ran out to the porch where her uncle watched endlessly for the onslaught. With smug pleasure, Margo realized that he had been looking in the wrong direction – that she had found the dragons living right here in town.

She touched Sibby's shoulder and, practically dancing with excitement, faced her uncle.

"I found them," she said.

He scowled and dropped the binoculars to his lap. "What are you yapping about?" he demanded.

"I found them, Uncle Daniel – the dragons."

The only sound was Sibby singing under her breath, the chalk's soft swish on paper, the distant scream of seagulls.

"I found the dragons," Margo repeated. "Here, in town...disguised as people. Trying to take over...sneaking in..."

"You found *the dragons?*" Her uncle demanded as if someone had hit him over the head, as if his brain was buzzing and he couldn't focus.

Margo nodded impatiently. "Yes. They're disguised as people – don't some of the old records say they can change their shapes? Move like people and sneak into the towns that way?"

"I heard it..." Uncle Daniel said slowly, "... but I never believed it. You sure?" He squinted at her.

"Yes, I'm sure. I saw it today. This witch, Addie Medway...I've known something was weird about her since they moved into town... right during school she started glowing all silver, and her eyes changed – looked like silver slits – not normal at all." Margo's breath quickened with excitement. "Her brother stopped her before she could change completely, but I saw it. I recognized it. They can't hide from us any more, Uncle Daniel. We got them!"

She watched the glow lighten her uncle's watery eyes. He reached out and gripped her arm tightly. "You did fine, Margo. All that studying and training I made you do is going to pay off. We'll get those snakes. Where's your brother?"

Margo frowned. "I don't know. Baseball practice maybe. He didn't see it – I did."

"And you played your part well," her uncle assured her. "But we need to get Ryan here. Start making plans for the hunt."

"I've got some ideas..." Margo started.

Her uncle waved a dismissive hand. "You've done your part. We need Ryan here."

Margo stepped back as if she'd been slapped. "Uncle Daniel," she managed, "I'm a St. George. I found them and I'm ready to deal with them."

Her uncle looked irritated. "You're just a girl, Margo. A smart one. But we need Ryan for this – it's what he was born to do."

"He was born to it? What about me?" Margo demanded. "I trained as hard as him and I studied more than he did – because he never studied anything."

Uncle Daniel's mouth quirked affectionately. "He wasn't much for learning. You might have to give him a few pointers, Margo. We have to support the hunt." His face suddenly got hard and he slapped his motionless legs. "Tips are all we can give him. I ought to be able to hunt along with him, but those snakes did this to me. But we'll pay 'em back good. They won't get away this time."

He picked up the binoculars and, hands shaking, stared out at the ocean again.

"They aren't out there," Margo spat. She turned and almost stumbling, made her way back into the house and up to her bedroom. She threw herself onto her bed. In silent, screaming rage, she pounded and pounded on her pillow.

She barely noticed when Sibby edged into the room, laid a sheaf of pictures on her desk, and then tiptoed away.

When Margo couldn't lie there any longer, she swung her legs off the bed, and jumped down to the floor. Aching with rage, she went down to the training yard and began her workout. Warm ups. Weights lifted. Obstacles jumped. Dozens of reps...pulling herself up on bars and rings, balancing on slanted walls, leaping across a series of beams. Her muscles swelled and her steps were light. Maybe Ryan had bulkier muscles, but she was more nimble and a whole lot smarter. Ryan had refused to spar with her for more than two years now, because despite his biceps, she used skill and brains to beat him every time.

She was the real warrior.

After an hour, panting, dripping sweat, Margo left the yard and went to soak in a hot shower. She heard Ryan come in and knew he and Uncle Daniel would be head to head, making the plans that she apparently had no place in. Good thing she was in the shower, because Margo despised tears. Despised any kind of weakness. She hadn't spent her life training, just to get all soppy.

Not now. Not when it was getting real.

When she came out, Sibby had curled up on her own bed, blankets shielding her from the world. The intensity of Uncle Daniel's hunt was probably too much. Abruptly, the anger drained out of Margo. Rapidly, she pulled on her clothes and went to sit beside her sister, unwrapping the blankets enough to expose Sibby's head. Margo smoothed her sister's tangled hair gently.

"Hey, it's okay, brat. I've got this." Margo kept her voice low and sing-song. "You know I won't let anything hurt you. I'm the strongest, toughest St. George that ever was. And I got a mission, brat. My mission is to keep people safe. And you're the most important person ever, so I promise I'll keep you safe."

As she stroked her sister's hair, Sibby's arm pushed out from the blankets and pointed like a compass needle toward the desk.

Frowning, Margo left the bed and went over to pick up Sibby's drawings.

Her heart began beating so hard she could hardly breathe. Scenes...smells and sounds clutched her, dragged her into the living reality of Sibby's pictures.

The first...a silvery-blue dragon lies crumpled on the ground. It moans piteously. A man stands irresolute between the dragon and two hunters as rain and wind howl around them. The earth heaves, the ground gives way, and the two men fall down into the ocean....

The second...a scream of pain. Margo pants, fighting a dragon by the shore. Her rage fills the page as she twists the dragon's leg and it cries out in anguish. Addie's scream reverberates through her....

The third...the crash of breaking branches as her brother, Ryan, and his friends barrel through woods, guns held high. Harsh breathing...pounding...screaming...

The fourth...a dragon rising into the sky; below lies the bleeding form of Jim Medway, Addie and Jacob's father.

The fifth...icy spray and heaving waves. Herself, Jacob, Sibby and the prostrate form of Dr. Medway fighting to keep a boat afloat in a surging surf. Above them, a silver dragon soars into the clouds.

The sixth...Cold. Fear. Howls. A grey blur of waves and ghostly reptilian forms...

The papers drift from Margo's icy hands... bitter cold envelopes her...is this death? Is she dying? Screams and howls reverberate in the air above. Echoes slide over freezing ocean waves. Her arms are weak...she has to hold on... pain is everywhere...is she dying?

With a low cry, Margo wrenched herself from Sibby's visions. Gasping, shaking, she looked over at her sister. Only Sibby's eyes could be seen, staring urgently from the blankets.

"Find the boat," her sister whispered. "Margo, you have to find your daddy's boat."

"This is crazy," Margo hissed. "This can't happen. Sibby...what have you seen?"

Her sister pulled the blankets over her head again. The mound shook as her body trembled violently, but her voice came out clearly. "You have to find the boat, Margo. Or it'll be too late!"

FOURTEEN

BRING IT ON

JACOB

School had ended, but Jacob was still waiting outside Principal Cartwright's office. As the minutes ticked by, he tried not to scream or swear. Terror and rage warred equally, sending tremors through his weak frame. Even as the teacher had hauled him off Addie's unconscious form, he had fought and yelled that they couldn't take his sister to the emergency room, that they had to get his father.

Somehow he had made them listen.

Addie had almost roused, mumbled that she wanted to go home. The school nurse had rushed down to the classroom with a wheel chair, and while Jacob stood panting, had lifted his sister into it and whisked her away. The principal had come, and gripping Jacob's arm tightly, escorted him from the room. His classmates had watched silently, staring as though he had turned into a freak.

Jacob didn't care. Addie now lay half-conscious on a bed in the nurse's office. Safe for the moment.

Jacob hung his head down, elbows resting on his knees, trying to calm the shudders still racing through his body. Addie had both bracelets on her arms. Unless someone pulled them off, he was sure...almost sure...that their magic would prevent her from transforming again.

How much had everyone seen?

What if the magic in the bracelets wasn't strong enough?

He groaned softly, partly from the pain of what he had forced his weak body to do, partly from the memory of the greedy exultation on Margo St. George's face.

"She knows," he whispered. His mind was slamming together the story of how his mother had met his father, the fervor of Margo's claim of being the last of the St. Georges. He now was terrifyingly sure that her family had been the hunters who had tried to kill his mother.

Margo had seen Addie's magical glow.

Margo would get it – she would discover their secret.

Margo would call out the hunt and the St. Georges would try to kill Addie.

Jacob's breath pounded. Unaccustomed rage streamed through his veins. He had to protect Addie. His family had to leave this place, go somewhere safe. He flexed his shaking arms, testing what little strength he had left. They had to run for their lives. He had to convince his father to take them and run.

"Can I get you anything?" Mrs. Cordova, the office manager interrupted the passions that were overwhelming him.

A second...then two...Jacob shook his head to clear his thoughts. Somehow, he forced a smile to his face. "No...I'm good," he muttered.

Her eyebrows arched. "I don't think we're doing good today," she said. "Really, Jacob, of all the kids in this school, I would never have expected such behavior from you. We're lucky Addie didn't break something. You don't fight like that at home, do you?"

"N..no...I..I d..don't know h..how it h..appened..." The words twisted in his mouth. He felt like everything inside him was on ramped up speed. "C..can I s..see Ad..die?"

Mrs. Cordova frowned. "Considering what you just did, I think that's a very bad idea. She's resting. Once your father gets here, I think she'll have to be checked out by a doctor."

The office manager slapped a file down on her desk. "I think you'll both have to be checked out by a doctor."

Jacob bowed his head again, the woman's anger and disappointment another weight to carry. He clenched his fists. Really, he didn't give a crap. There was so much more at stake than whether his "*What a great kid!*" image had been shattered.

They had no idea what he was really like.

No idea what he was facing.

The principal's door opened just as his father hurried into the office. The tightly controlled anxiety on his dad's face and the serious frown on Cartwright's, further aroused Jacob's sense of danger. He considered and abandoned the idea of putting on his "great kid" persona. With all the emotions coursing through him, he didn't think he could keep it up anyway. He'd never felt less like a good kid in his life. It was a relief to let it go, to let the slow simmer of his fury surge through him.

"Addie?" his father asked.

"She's lying down in the nurse's office," Principal Cartwright said. "She seems fine although we wanted to take her to emergency. Jacob insisted that you wouldn't allow that. And," he added reluctantly, "somehow we never got your paperwork. I was forced to go along with Jacob."

Dr. Medway looked at his son, his air of bewilderment intensifying. "What happened?"

Jacob pulled himself to his feet, stifling a groan of pain as he let the crutches hold his weight. "It's a s..seizure...like m..mom used to h...have..." *Understand,* he pleaded silently. *Please, please understand.*

"We're at a complete loss here," the principal interjected. "The teacher said Addie was starting to act strangely during her presentation and then Jacob," he paused to look sorrowfully at the boy, "Jacob attacked her."

"A seizure?" Dr. Medway stared at his son.

"L..like m...mom..." Jacob held his father's eyes. Desperate. "I..I thought a..a phys..ical sh..shock...like when you slap s..someone in hyster..rics would m..make her st..stop."

"That's not how it works, son," the principal said. "That was an incredibly foolhardy thing to do."

"Like your mother..." his father said slowly. "Like your mother?"

"J..just li..ike m..mom."

Dr. Medway passed a hand over his forehead and rubbed his eyes. "It's not..." he started and stopped.

“We n..need to take Ad..die h..home,” Jacob insisted. “Now!”

“Yes…yes we do,” his father said abruptly. “Mr. Cartwright, I do need to get my children home. Especially Addie.”

“But…”

“I understand if you need to interview Jacob. Tomorrow,” Dr. Medway interrupted. “I’ll take Addie to my specialist who…who understands her condition.” He put out his hand to shake the principal’s hand. “And I’ll call you in the morning.”

The principal gave way. “Addie’s in the health room. The next door on the right. I’ll be expecting your call.”

Still frowning, he returned to his office. Mrs. Cardova watched them with skeptically raised brows, but Jacob didn’t care. His dad helped him adjust his crutches and together they headed to the nurse’s office.

Addie lay stretched out on a paper-covered cot. Her eyes looked exhausted, almost bruised. Jacob wondered who, of the two of them, would look the most beat up. Addie had fought back ferociously. Pinning her in class had been crazy stupid, but it was all he could think of to do.

Not that I was thinking, he told himself. Why hadn’t he grasped that Addie could change in front of everyone like that? *Because school is boring*, he realized. *And Addie has to have something that makes her angry or excited.*

"Hey, bro," his sister whispered, "no fair sneaking up on me like that."

"How else am I g..going to bring you down?" Jacob countered.

Addie laughed weakly, and forced herself to a sitting position. "I think I need to go home, Dad," she told their father.

Dr. Medway nodded and offered his arm to support her. "Are you alright?"

Addie shook her head and for a moment Jacob saw tears glisten in her eyes. "No, I don't think so."

The ride home in the truck was silent. Squished between them, Addie barely moved. Jacob saw that she kept her eyes closed most of the way. He wondered uneasily if he had broken or badly bruised anything when he had tackled his sister. But what else was he supposed to do?

Their father kept all his attention on the road, his knuckles white on the steering wheel. When they got home, he pulled the truck up as close to the door as he could, then hurried out to offer an arm to Jacob and then Addie. For once, Jacob was glad of support. Addie didn't shake it off either.

Without speaking they settled in the living room, Addie sagging on the sofa, Jacob and his dad on chairs, all facing each other.

Their father cleared his throat. "Do you... do you want some tea?"

"Not so much," Addie snapped. She shoved back her hair that had tangled and flopped across her forehead. "I want some answers. What...what is happening to me?"

Dr. Medway twisted the wedding ring on his finger and hesitated. Jacob again felt himself stiffening in anxiety.

"Dad?" Addie demanded.

"I...my best guess," he said, dropping his hands, "is that you are more like your mother than either of us knew."

"Mom knew," Jacob interrupted. "She t..told me to look after Addie. W..warned me the bracelets w..would keep her from l..losing it."

Their father nodded. "Audra tried to tell me, but I didn't want to hear – didn't want to think about what you two might have to face." He scrubbed his fist across his forehead. "I know too much about the fates of dragons. Your mother told me that the European dragon purges drove the clans into hiding decades...centuries ago. Some clans chose to enhance their shape-shifting capabilities and live with humans. Fascinating really." His eyes brightened for an instant with a scholar's passion, then dulled as he looked at his children. "Her clan came here with the Vikings a thousand years ago to escape the hunts. They avoid humans – won't have anything to do with them. They kill anyone that finds their hidden caves." His smile faltered. "A bit blood-thirsty, really. Rather justifies some of the mythology."

"Then wh..why did mom marry you?" Jacob demanded. "Did you p..put a spell on her or..or something?"

Dr. Medway looked startled. "A spell? I wouldn't know how. We…um…fell in love."

"Wh..what?" Jacob tried to beat down his revulsion. Human. Non-human. Boring, ordinary world. Magical and extraordinary existence.

And his parents? *Gross.*

"Then why did she leave?" Addie demanded. "If she loved us so much." Jacob heard the frightened scorn in her voice.

"She couldn't keep human form any longer. She was burning up inside," their father said. "I would have gone with her to the clan, but she thought her dragon kin would kill me. And she was terrified they would go berserk that she had born half-breed offspring."

The twins stared at their father in horror. "Are they rabid ani..animals?" Jacob demanded.

"They are wild dragons," he said almost apologetically, "and have avoided humans for ten centuries."

"Mom w..was one of them – and she was full of love!" Jacob protested.

"Yes," Dr. Medway said eagerly, "yes, she was. And the dragons are ancient and wise, and the last carriers of magic in our rather mundane world. But...apparently rather bigoted."

"That's just fabulous." Addie jumped up, scowling. She began pacing back and forth.

Jacob watched her. He didn't trust her energy, could almost feel the dragon rage building within her.

She gestured widely, angrily. "And where does that leave us? Caught between the crazy dragon slayers as represented by the marvelous Margo St. George, or our blood-thirsty relatives hiding out somewhere and eating anyone they don't like?"

"They don't eat them," Dr. Medway protested. "They're wild, not barbaric."

"Well, that's relief," Addie snarled.

"Dad," Jacob snapped, "this isn't some academic research. Addie is turning into a dragon!"

His father and twin froze as though they had just realized the obvious.

"We have to..to leave here," Jacob yelled. "What were y..you thinking, bringing us h..here?"

"I thought...I thought your mother might come back," their father said. "It's where I found her...."

"It's where the c..crazy people tried to kill her," Jacob shouted. "D..did you think about that...or..or us?"

Silence. Dr. Medway stared at the wall, color fading from his face. "I suspect I haven't been thinking clearly at all."

Addie sank back onto the sofa, staring at her wrists. "So these bracelets are all that's keeping me from turning into a dragon? From diving head-long into magic?" She glanced scornfully at her father. "From going wild... but *not* barbaric." With a fast, jerky motion, she snapped the bracelets from her arms and dropped them on the table. A flush of excitement rose over her face. "Then, bring it on."

"Addie, no!" Jacob cried. But already, he knew it was too late.

FIFTEEN

THE BRIDGE ACROSS THE ABYSS

ADDIE

At first nothing seemed to happen. Addie and her twin stared across the room at each other, chests heaving. Addie felt a prickling across her skin as she gulped in air, gasping a little like she had been holding her breath for too long. The oxygen sent a whoosh of heat through her, warmth that felt like standing by a roaring fire after being out in the bitter cold.

She laughed.

The dizzying sensations she'd felt before rushed over her, but this time she didn't black out, didn't fall into the pit that lay between the two separate strands of her heritage. Instead, Addie felt strength surge upward into her being, felt the chasm narrow, and then as though her spirit finally understood, she stepped across the abyss that had torn her apart.

It was so simple.

Strength rippled through her. The silver on her fingernails spread outward to silver her skin, not scaly or metallic, but silken, shining like rich satin in the dull light of their living room. Her eyesight sharpened so that she could see the drops of moisture forming on her brother's forehead and the color draining from her father's cheeks. Her other senses heightened too. She could hear her family's quickened breathing, the soft cry that died in her brother's throat. The acrid smell of their emotions overlaying the salt tang that always hung in the air.

She felt whole, complete...powerful.

And cramped. The living room seemed too small, too faded, too removed from the vibrancy of the living world. Barely aware of the change in her form, her body somehow shaped itself to match the contours of the room and then the small door as Addie slipped out of the confines of their house.

Behind her, Jacob and her father cried out, but she was drunk with the smells, sounds and tastes of the world outside. She heard the whisper of wind soughing through the evergreen boughs, smelled the salty tang in the gusting air, tasted a thousand lives large and small that surrounded her. It was as if the earth itself breathed and she could breathe in harmony with it. Reality spread before her in brilliant layers that she had never before perceived.

Addie laughed and stretched her wings. Could she launch skyward? Would she simply know how to fly or would it be like a toddler taking her first steps?

"*Addie!*"

Jacob stood before her, tears streaming down his face, his hands awkwardly pulling at her arm. What did he want her to do? She felt a surge of affection for her twin...would have answered, but there was a whisper in her mind. A voice snaking through her awareness. No... not one voice...many voices. Ancient voices. Reaching to her...calling to her...offering her the heritage of her kind.

Welcome, daughter. We have waited long for your coming....

I'm here! Addie gasped, sudden joy rushing through her veins. She reached out with her thoughts as easily as she would have reached with her hands. *I'm here!*

And then a different voice howled into her. Ancient. Cracked with madness. And then, not one vicious voice. A mob. A cacophony of anger. Close by. Dragging her from the welcoming voices. Hunting her, probing her thoughts. Ransacking her being. Searching for her....

"No!" Addie shrieked.

Nipping, biting, gouging her mind. Fraying the new magic that had awakened her. Wounding...destroying her.

Help me! she screamed.

"*Addie!*" Somehow Jacob's voice pierced the fury of the onslaught.

Addie keened in terror, searching this way and that across unfamiliar voids of existence. The hunters clawed and harried her.

She had to escape, become human again... but she didn't know how to find herself.

Help me, Jacob....

And then she saw it. A sapphire blue light. Flickering, calling. Not strong, but Addie knew that light. Desperately, she fled towards it, breaking through the raging minds that pummeled her into death.

Into non-existence.

Jacob, she cried again, knowing her strength was nearly gone. Somehow her brother reached to her from the weakness of his human self...if she could touch her twin....

A flare of silvery blue light suddenly blazed up between Addie and the hunters. Heart near bursting, she reeled across the void toward her brother's blue flame. A bridge she could cross, but the howling voices could not.

As she dove back into human form, the voices dwindled. But like an echo, she heard her mother shriek as the hunters turned on her.

And then silence.

For the second time that day, Addie fought her way back to consciousness. She lay on the sodden grass behind their home. Jacob and her father knelt on either side of her, rain splattering down on them all. They were calling her, but she couldn't quite understand the words. Tears ran from her father's eyes. Jacob's body shuddered with spasms. Above them, black branches waved in the restless wind. Clouds rolled in from the unquiet ocean. Crows shrieked storm warnings.

Addie's couldn't stop the sobs that shook her.

"A..addie..." Jacob gasped. He held her hand tightly. Dimly, she was aware that he had never let go of her dragon hand while the hordes hunted her. A trickle of blood dripped from a gash in his cheek. She must have done that.

Struggling to sit up, feeling like all her stamina, magical or otherwise, had drained away, Addie gripped her brother's hand, still gathering strength from him, feeling how the connection between them made both stronger. With her other hand, she tried to wipe the water from her face, tears and raindrops mixed.

"So I guess that wasn't such a good idea after all," she managed to gasp out.

"T..told you," Jacob whispered. He was breathing hard; the rain slicked his hair to his forehead and his slight body shook with spasms.

Her father gathered Addie up in his arms and hugged her, rocking her like she was still the toddler who had run to him for comfort. She clung to him as he carried her back into the house, settled her on the sofa, and brought towels for her and her brother. Even as the warmth seeped back into her bones, no matter how hard she willed it, Addie couldn't stop shuddering.

How could this have happened? How could she have flamed into such strength only to be nearly destroyed by a thunder of dragons? How could her own mother have been spawned in such savagery? What did that make her? Would more than her shape change?

Addie forced herself to towel her hair, dry her face...not allow the sobs to escape again. She was better than this. She, Addie Medway, would not be beaten...not even by dragons. Not even by her own treacherous DNA.

Jacob hadn't moved, had barely dried his face. She reached out and gripped his arm, now trying to will some crumbs of her pitiful strength back into him. What had it cost him to find her? He wasn't a dragon...couldn't call on the magical strength she'd had. What good had all this done her...?

"I saw Mom," she said.

Jacob raised his head, eyes startled. Their father stilled.

"She...she's alive." Addie's voice quavered. "She saved me from them. I think they may have..." The words tangled in her throat. Dimly Addie realized that as she settled back into her human self, those other realities were fading, becoming less certain.

But she *knew*. Her mother had found her, saved her from...whatever those dragon things really were.

Addie's voice throbbed with passion. "I thought she was dead. That she *had* to be dead or she would've come back to us."

"I t..told you she's not dead," Jacob insisted. His fists opened and closed. "She just...had to l..leave."

"Leave us for them?" Addie demanded. "They turned on her...the dragons. They tried to kill me! She could be dead because of me."

"No, Adara!" Her father stood up abruptly. "They...they don't kill their own," he said. "Exile perhaps...but not kill."

"They were trying to kill me!" Addie shouted. "There was no exile or chasing away. They were trying to murder me...and they would have, if Mom and Jacob hadn't helped me."

Their father passed a hand over his face, his body swaying a little. "I think...I think we need some tea."

"Like tea will fix things," Addie snarled.

"We need to sit down...think calmly and rationally...." He disappeared into the kitchen.

"He's wrong," she said fiercely to Jacob. "They would've killed me. There was one especially...but they all would have killed me."

"May..maybe they d..don't think you're one of th..them," Jacob said helplessly. He reached for the bracelets. "P..put these back on, Addie. Please."

She stared at them, revulsion building in her. The runes engraved in the silver seemed menacing now. "I can't...I won't. They're like a straight-jacket, keeping me from myself."

"But if you sh..shift again," he pleaded. "The St. G..georges are crazy...and the dragons..."

Addie struggled to her feet. "I don't care. I'm going to take a nap...recruit my strength.

I need to be ready for when the next set of crazies try to murder me."

Forcing back the shuddering sobs that threatened her still, Addie stomped up to her bedroom. No way she could sleep after that waking nightmare. But how was she going to save herself? Wearily, Addie sat on the side of the bed and looked around her room.

She had never before felt so small and weak.

SIXTEEN

POOLS OF BLOOD

MARGO

No one, especially Margo, was surprised that the Medway twins didn't show up for school the next day. She stared bitterly at Addie's empty seat in Myths class, sat sullenly through the next round of stupid student presentations, and contemptuously ignored the excited gossip that rippled through the school.

Only she knew the truth.

But what was she going to do about it?

As she wove her way through the hallways, she caught sight of her brother in the center of a knot of open-mouthed idiots. Margo shoved her way through in time to hear Ryan announce, "Yeah, those Medways are cursed. Y'know, shapeshifters like on TV." He threw back his shoulders. "But I got this. I've been trained. So who's with me?"

Margo slammed him between the shoulder blades. "Shut up!" she hissed. "Just shut up, you moron!"

Ryan swiveled, anger reddening his face. He shoved back. "Butt out, Margo. This is man's work. My work!"

"You don't know..." Margo tried to say, but Ryan's buddy, Sean, shouldered her out of the circle. Everyone laughed while Margo stood, fists clenched, on the outside of the crowd. For a brief moment, she considered ripping their collective heads off, or at least laying them out with a lot of bruises. Those muscle-bound idiots were too stupid to know that she could do it too.

But what good would that do? Ryan had already said too much. Shown so clearly that he had no idea what their family heritage actually meant. That a crusade to save the people wasn't a golden opportunity for him to brag and flex his muscles.

"Stupid...idiotic...moron," Margo snarled as she strode away from the crowd of fools. The halls echoed with Ryan's loud exhortation, "*So who's with me?*"

"Margo, did you hear...?" Karla interrupted her thoughts.

"Shut up!" Margo snapped, and kept going. Right out the side door of the school. She started running toward the shielding trees and restless shoreline. She had to get away from the twisted gossip, exaggerated rumors, and the realization that these idiots, led by her moron brother, would never understand what had happened in their run-down town.

She jogged hard, leapt over driftwood, danced back from waves, threw punches and kicks at imaginary enemies.

Avoided thinking about what this really meant.

Finally, miles later, when she couldn't run any more, Margo sank down onto a pile of driftwood logs, sinking her head into her hands. What if Ryan roused the dragons and they came after her family? The old records were full of the serpents' savagery, their relentless attacks on the innocent – innocents like Sibby.

Ryan didn't have a clue and his friends were worse. They'd flex their muscles, brandish some kind of weapons, and make a lot of noise.

And then they'd run.

Or die.

Margo fought back a sob. More than the St. George family fortune had shrunk to almost nothing. Their history...their skills... their purpose had all become a joke.

There were mythic dragons in her town and she had thought that running around a homemade training yard made her ready to face them. Terror surged through her veins and she nearly threw up. It was hopeless. Her ancestors had been experienced warriors, knights who studied their enemies closely and prepared their whole lives to fight them.

And even then, a lot of them were killed.

Margo pushed herself to her feet. Her family had to escape. She had to get Sibby and her mom away from here before Ryan and their crazy uncle brought disaster on them all. There were police and soldiers a lot better equipped to fight the monsters when they appeared.

She had to get her family away. Now. Before it was too late.

Margo groaned and wearily began jogging back toward her home. It was at least eight miles, even by road. Why had she run so far? What had she been thinking?

How could she save them if she didn't use her brain?

Shame nearly overwhelmed her until she remembered she was a St. George. "You may be one of the last," she panted. "But you're still a dragon slayer, Margo. It's up to you whether you'll be a hero or a coward."

The miles slowly disappeared under her feet. She would not give up. Not ever. Her breathing was labored and her muscles ached, but she didn't stop running. Throwing open the door, she staggered into the hallway. Her mom was chattering away to a client in the living room hair salon, but Margo pushed in anyway.

"Mom," Margo interrupted. "The dragons are real. They're coming. We have to get away!"

Color surged up her mother's neck and into her tired face. "That's not funny, Margo." She turned her shoulder and fluffed her customer's hair. "Kids," she offered with a forced laugh, "they don't get what's funny and what isn't."

Mrs. Newsom patted her curls. "I like how you've cut it this time..."

"Mom!" Margo pleaded.

"Enough, Margo." Her mom's eyes snapped with anger.

Giving up, Margo backed out of the room. Her mom had never believed in the St. George crusades. Her husband had, and he had died. The family legacy had cost her mom everything.

Would it cost them even more?

For a moment, Margo stood in the hallway, clenching and unclenching her teeth. Exhaustion made her want to cry in frustration, but she wouldn't give in to that any more than she would surrender to her aching muscles. Instead, she squared her shoulders and went out onto the porch.

Sibby had been relegated to a small corner of the picnic table because Uncle Daniel had covered the surface with maps, charts, and scribbled notes. Excitement had given his eyes an unnatural glitter as he glanced up at his niece.

"I'm thinking we can drive 'em up the bluff and pick 'em off here," he said. His finger jabbed a spot on a contour map that showed the town's terrain. "Ryan's already recruiting a posse to corner them." He laughed harshly. "We got them worms...we got 'em!"

"Uncle Daniel," Margo said desperately, "Ryan and his friends don't know how to fight dragons. They'll be...hurt...." She swallowed, finding the words hard to say. "We've got to escape. Go to Halifax. Tell the army or something."

Her uncle lifted his eyes from the map and stared at her. "What are you saying?" he demanded. "You may be a girl, but you're a St. George...and no St. George's ever been a coward!"

"I'm not a coward," Margo snapped. "I'm just not crazy. What do we know about fighting dragons? One...just one...killed my father and crippled you. Do we know how many there are? Does Ryan know how to do anything except brag and bully? We have to get away! The stories...."

"The stories don't ever say nothin' about a St. George running and hiding," her uncle jeered. "I'm a cripple and you don't see me trying to run." His lip curled as he stared at her. "I'm ashamed we have the same name."

He turned away, gathering a handful of charts into his lap and picking up his binoculars to stare out to sea. "Ashamed..." he muttered.

Margo leaned on the table, fighting for control. Her eyes strayed over to Sibby, still drawing as if a quarrel hadn't raged around her.

"Oh, Sibby," Margo gently stroked her sister's hair, her mind frantically forming and discarding plan after plan.

Her sister moved under her hand as she pointed to the drawing she had been working on. Margo nearly stopped breathing. She recognized the bluff behind the Medway's house, and she could make out the shadowed figures of Ryan and his friends, a wrecked wheelchair on the grass, and a body sprawled in the dirt.

But all across the page were smears and pools of red blood.

Sibby looked up at her, eyes filling with tears. "You have to find the boat," she whispered. "Sail away...."

Margo stared down at her sister. Sibby's pictures had been right all along. Her mom didn't believe her; her brother and uncle were crazy with blood lust. Margo had no money to catch a bus...but if she could find her father's boat, she and Sibby could sail away, up the coast toward Halifax. They would be safe there, away from her crazy uncle and stupid brother. Away from the dragons.

Margo took a deep breath and eyed their uncle. She schooled her voice to mask the screaming emotions tearing through her. "Uncle Daniel," she said, "if we had my dad's boat we could come at them from the water too, not just the land."

"I can't swim, dummy," her uncle said. "I ain't getting into no sailboat."

Margo clenched her teeth. "No, you got to be running things from up here. But if the dragons tear up the road, we could get supplies round by the boat."

"Dragons are stupid animals. They ain't got the brains to ruin the road."

Margo wanted to scream. "Yeah...but if

the cars get hit with their...their fire breath...I know I can't do much, being a girl..." Margo hoped her uncle didn't hear the sarcasm. "... but I know how to sail. I could bring around any supplies you wanted."

Her uncle grunted.

"If I had Dad's old boat..."

There was a long silence. Margo wondered how loudly her uncle would scream if she shoved him off the side of the porch. It was a lovely picture in her mind.

"Boat may have rotted out," Uncle Daniel muttered at last. "There's a good-sized water cave down by the old place...about half a mile from where those Medways live. There's one big rock on top of the cliff, and a sort of path under it. Can't get in from the water 'cause of the surf. Your dad had a time buildin' it. Took years...told him it was stupid."

"How was he going to get it out to the water," Margo probed, "if the surf's so bad?"

"Me, I liked motor boats," Uncle Daniel mumbled. "They got power."

"My dad had to have a plan." Margo clenched her fists, fighting back frustration. "He must have had a way to sail the boat out, didn't he?"

Her uncle shrugged. "Told me he'd just float it out at high tide. Sounds crazy. But I ain't been there since that reptile broke my back. Boat's probably all rotten by now."

A smile of triumph lit Margo's face. She glanced down at Sibby. Her sister was drawing again...this time a shadowy boat, wrapped in canvas, perched on a wooden cradle above the rocks with lapping water below.

Margo touched her sister's unresponsive shoulder.

"Thanks, kid," she murmured. "I'm on it now."

SEVENTEEN

MAGIC IS ALL WE'VE GOT!

JACOB

If he could pace, Jacob knew he'd be pacing now. He had barely been able to sleep the night before – the day's nightmares had kept him awake. There had been no question of going to class. Principal Cartwright had phoned, but no one had bothered to answer. Even their father who had always loved routine and rules ignored the insistent calls from the school.

"D..don't you g..get this?" Jacob had flung at his father and sister. "W..we have to leave here. G..go away. Margo s..saw!"

"I'm not afraid of Margo," Addie said scornfully. She smacked a bowl of soup on the table in front of him.

"You sh..should be!" Jacob retorted and in

a spasm of anger, shoved the bowl away. The broth slopped onto the table.

No one paid any attention.

Hopelessly, Jacob mopped the liquid up with his paper napkin. He thought he'd throw up if he tried to eat.

Addie swiped peanut butter onto some bread and then sat on a stool, leaving it untouched before her.

"You should ea..eat," Jacob urged.

"Why?" his sister snapped. "So I have enough energy to maintain my freakdom?"

"That's not accurate," their father interrupted. The kettle whistled and he went to pour water into the teapot, then stopped.

"It's full, dad," Addie told him. "You made about six pots last night that nobody drank."

"Rather a waste of good tea," Dr. Medway murmured. He poured the cold tea into the sink, added more teabags to the pot, and then refilled it.

"And that's a metaphor for our lives," Addie muttered. She threw her sandwich into the trash and hunched down on the chair beside her brother.

Jacob leaned over and bumped her shoulder. She scowled more fiercely, but didn't twist away. Their father set mugs of sugary tea in front of them, and then, taking his own mug in one hand and clutching another pile of ancient books under his arm, disappeared back into his office.

"Y..you need to w..wear the bracelets." Jacob had been urging, begging, pleading with his twin all morning

"Give it up, Jacob," Addie snapped. "I won't do it! I'm not having my life controlled by our mother's stupid magic!"

"But y..you are m..magic!" His voice was growing tired with talking, and his stuttering was so bad, it wouldn't be long before even he wouldn't be able to make out his words. "Th.. the bracelet's m..magic is a..all w..we've got!"

"Leave me alone!" Addie screamed and jumped up from her chair. When a silver sheen began to roll across her skin, her face looked frightened...and then determined. Fists clenched, eyes tightly closed, Addie stood motionless as the glow subsided.

Forcing himself to breathe normally, Jacob reached out and touched her arm. This time she yanked it away, took a few steps back, then turned and ran up the stairs in the hallway. He heard her bedroom door slam.

Jacob realized he was shaking – that he was so angry with his twin, his father, and even his mother for doing nothing. Their lives were hanging by a thread – a thread controlled by old myths and Margo St. George. Disaster in the form of crazed mobs, exposure, maybe death loomed on their personal horizons and no one was doing anything to stop it.

Frustration and fury prickled under his skin, making him want to punch everyone.

Get real, Jacob, he snarled at himself. *If you try to fight, your useless body will and end up in a useless heap.*

But he shook with rage anyway.

Thrusting himself to his feet, he went into the living room and snapped the bracelets on his own wrists. In her mood right now, Addie might just throw them over the bluff into the ocean. They needed these gifts from their mother.

The bracelets were all they had.

Taking even such a small action soothed him. He studied the runes on the cuffs, wishing he could read them. But at least the feel of cool metal against his skin calmed him down some.

If nobody else in his family was doing anything, he had to. Even if he was completely pathetic, he had to try. Thinking had always been how he solved the problems that beset his life. Maybe this was no different.

No, he thought bitterly, this is a lot different. Before he'd had to fake being cool, figure out how to get down an inconvenient staircase, maybe make friends with someone who freaked out at his handicap. Never death. Never ancient magic. Never dragons or slayers.

Face it, he didn't have Addie's toughness or his father's knowledge. All he had was his own brain. Jacob hoped desperately that it wouldn't let him down.

Addie was still banging around in her bedroom upstairs, and their father would probably stay hidden behind his stack of books all day. Jacob decided he'd go seriously crazy if he stayed inside a minute longer. The sky had darkened and the air had the feel of another storm, but he didn't care.

With no regard for the probability of tumbling onto his head, Jacob stomped outside through the rank grass and weeds until he stood on the very edge of the bluff. At the horizon's edge, grey-black clouds scudded across the sky. Jacob thought he could make out lightning crackling in the distance.

The wind around him was fretful, tossing up leaves then dying down abruptly, only to gust angrily over the land again. Jacob leaned against a tree, letting his arm crutches fall to the ground. What would it be like to be on a boat out there? Feel the swells rising beneath the thin hull? And the noise! Jacob was sure the noise would be like a thundering train or a stadium full of roaring crowds.

The wind, the fear, all thrilled him, raced through his blood as though he had experienced it once before. He exulted in the wild feeling, the coursing of blood in his veins, the raw life of the world no longer masked by civilization.

It was as if he could lift upwards into the sky, soar on the storm, roar out his joy....

"Jacob?"

He slammed back to himself.

"Are you alright, son?" His father leaned to pick up the crutches and propped them back against the tree.

The wind made Jacob's eyes tear up... washed over him, taking away the wild thrill he had imagined.

"I..I'm good," he managed.

"About yesterday..." His father stood beside him, staring out at the ocean. White caps were surging over the surface now. "Are you sure...quite sure...that this Margo St. George recognized Addie for...for what she has inherited from your mother?"

"Yes." Jacob wanted to yell at his father but it seemed the emotions had all washed out of him. Instead, he too stared out at the ocean, watching the storm roll towards them.

“You’re very sure?” his father asked again.

Jacob pushed down his anger. “V..very.”

His father sighed. “Then I suppose we will need to leave after all.” He wiped a hand over his eyes. “There was a terrifying savagery to those men who hunted down your mother. I won’t expose Addie to that.” He gazed wearily across the water. “I had hoped Audra would come back. But instead, it seems hope led us into a trap.”

Not hope, Jacob thought bitterly. *Desperation. Thinking everything could be amazing. It grabs and won’t let go. And it got me too.*

He should have been making plans, thinking about how to save his sister. Instead, he’d just stood here, watching the storm roll closer and closer, letting himself fly into the fantasy that left his miserable body behind. By now, he should be used to the fact his body was broken and would never be fixed. But his mind would do anything he wanted.

He had to trust in his mind.

EIGHTEEN

PSYCHOTIC FIGMENTS OF IMAGINATION

ADDIE

"I can't believe I'm so stupid," Addie muttered. She looked at the disaster around her and sighed, all her rage worn out by the wanton destruction of her bedroom. Unless she planned to go totally dragon and find some nice comfy cave to curl up in, she would have to put the mattress back on the bed and pick up a few of the blankets she'd thrown around.

Dumping out her drawers hadn't been too smart either.

"And I'll bet such an incredible show of strength would terrify Margo and those Addie-eating dragons," she said bitterly. "If you mess with me, Margo St. George, I might throw a T-shirt at you. And dragons, I've got a whole arsenal of balled up sweat socks."

As she wearily put her room back into some semblance of order, Addie's mind skittered around her actions. Sure, she'd always had a temper. But this unchecked fury? This was crazy stuff.

Maybe she'd learned the hard way to keep herself from slipping into a dragon body, but were dragon rages taking over her mind anyway? What if she went feral or something and turned on Jacob and her father?

Addie slammed the drawer back into her dresser. She couldn't hide in her room forever.

Kicking the door shut on the mess behind her, Addie called out to her brother. Nothing. He wasn't the type to ignore her, so after a quick sweep of the house, she went out the kitchen door and made her way to the bluff. The wind was tossing leaves around, filling her lungs with sharp, cool air. Addie lifted her arms in joy at the roiling elements.

Then, remembering how this had swept her away before, she dropped her hands and yanked her mind back under control. "Bad Addie Dragon," she admonished herself.

She spotted her brother and father then, partially hidden by the tough spruce trees, standing by the bluff overlooking the sea. In bitter embarrassment, she hesitated and then lifting her chin, walked over.

"Family picnic?" she asked.

Her father looked puzzled when they turned toward her, but Jacob's smile tilted up the corners of his mouth. Without realizing she'd been holding it, Addie let out a long breath.

"Storm's c..coming," Jacob said.

Addie shrugged and stood beside him so that their shoulders touched. "Real or metaphor?"

He laughed then. "B..both."

"I've gone through all my books," their father said. "Several times. None of my resources say anything about dragon children, but I can't believe that you two would be the very first." Exhaustion greyed his face. "We need your mother to help us sort this out."

"Well, that's another thing she bailed out on, isn't it?" Addie snapped.

"Addie..." their dad began.

"Don't, just don't, talk to me right now!" She turned on her heel and strode away from them. Maybe hurling some stones into the heaving waves would relieve the dragon rage pounding through her.

But when she reached the beach, the desire to throw herself into meaningless activity abruptly drained away. Instead, she sank down onto a log and watched the way the wind whipped the waves into crests that smashed over the beach.

Like me, she thought. *Dragon DNA and Margo St. George and my AWOL mother are driving me into a frenzy that will kill me. But I won't let them win. So, get control of yourself, Addie Medway.*

Somehow, she had figured out how to manage the shape shifting. Maybe the next step was to get a handle on the fire that kept erupting in her brain.

Just think, Addie, she told herself, *maybe you don't have to be completely insane.*

Determinedly, nervously, Addie began poking into the far corners of her own mind. And it was terrifying. How could she never have sensed the dragon thoughts lurking behind the bubble of what she'd accepted as her real self?

Had her dragon nature been asleep until now? Or had she unconsciously hidden it away?

But why now? Why was she turning into some weird mutant dragon girl, just like the wildest comic book story?

"Addie Medway," she shouted over the rising wind. "By day an ordinary teenager – by night, the terrifying Dragon Girl."

She wanted to cry. The jokes weren't helping at all, not when she was scared right down to her silver toenails. Toenails that were getting sopping wet from the wind-whipped spray. Like the rest of her.

She should go in and get out of the elements.

But there was no place to hide from the elements erupting within her.

Taking a deep breath, Addie settled firmly onto the driftwood log and slid into her core self. It was like standing at a safe distance to study some alien creature from a sci fi movie. A swirling grey and silver cloud growing bigger and bigger behind her everyday thoughts.

Mesmerized, she mentally poked at it.

At first, nothing. Then as she touched it again, conversations clattered in her mind, like her phone slipping in and out of a reception area. Snippets of something... words... memories... knowledge, began to seep into her awareness. The words seemed storm-tossed, caught on thrusting currents of air. It was as though she looked at a forgotten photo and slowly remembered the day it had been taken. Flashes of images, colors, sounds, smells...slowly sliding together to form a whole memory.

"*Daughter...we wait for you!*" pleaded the distant gentle voices.

"No!" Addie cried and yanked herself back. Trembling, she huddled on the roaring beach, blowing sand stinging her skin. She remembered how those voices had started before, all warm and loving...and then another screaming voice had drowned them out, and the dragons had tried to kill her. She was still shaking when Jacob found her.

"You shouldn't come down here," she said. "Not without me...in case you fall." Her voice trembled.

Jacob sank down on the log beside her. "I.. it's amazing what I c..can do when I h..have to," he muttered. He slung his arm around her shoulder and she leaned into him. "W..won't let you f..fall either, Addie."

"Not having fun, brother," she whispered. "The dragon stuff keeps grabbing me."

Struggling to speak over the keening wind, she told him then about the voices calling to her. "I don't know if they're in my head...like I'm totally crazy...or if I'm somehow talking to other dragons. Some okay ones that aren't trying to kill me. Or if it's a trick and they're all really trying to murder me."

"C..can you ask?" he said.

"You're nuts," Addie retorted but had to laugh. "*Excuse me, psychotic figment of my imagination, is this just a friendly chat or are you trying to destroy me?"*

When her brother laughed too, Addie suddenly felt better. No matter what, she wasn't alone in this. Even if he wasn't a dragon, Jacob would always have her back.

"Dad's right. We n..need Mom," he said abruptly. "Maybe she c..can explain."

"Let's just phone her," Addie snapped.

Jacob sighed and stared moodily out at the heaving water. "We know she's a..live because she saved you. Maybe there is a w..way to find her."

"We should go in, before the storm gets worse," Addie said. The fear of the dragon savagery constricted her throat. "I...I don't think I can face the dragons...not even to find Mom," she managed.

Jacob nodded. "D..dad might know."

Addie stood up and brushed wet sand from her jeans. "If he knew how to find Mom," she argued, "he already would have done it."

Jacob also heaved himself to his feet, using his crutches to brace himself against the wind. Addie put out a hand to steady him.

"I'm not scared of those voices," Addie defended herself. She smiled bitterly. "Just terrified."

"I h..have an idea," he told her and began stumping through the sand toward the steps up the bluff.

Addie walked behind him, ready to catch her brother if he fell on the wet steps. But as usual, despite the unwieldiness he fought with, he didn't slip. Not once.

Please, have a good plan, Addie thought desperately. *Because I don't have any ideas at all.*

Gratefully, she followed Jacob into the house. A dragon could probably knock the building over and burn it down in two minutes. But for the moment, it felt blissfully warm and safe.

NINETEEN

THE LAST WARRIOR

MARGO

Despite the storm growling fitfully up from the ocean, Margo threw on her jacket and headed out. Using her uncle's maps, she had done her best to pinpoint the location of the hidden cave where her father had stashed his boat sixteen years before.

Her mom had always said her dad was careful, not like her half-crazy uncle. That's why she'd left her home in Alaska, because her new husband had promised to look after everything. But it hadn't worked so well, she'd added bitterly.

Margo prayed that her long-dead father had built the boat right. That he'd made the sailboat weather-proof. That she could make it sea-worthy. That it would save Sibby and her mom from the dragons that were coming.

Her muscles ached from her earlier crazed run, but she couldn't let that stop her. The grumbling storm lashed rain across her face and drove water through her thin jacket. Bitterly Margo wished there was enough money in their family to buy a decent coat. Good thing this wasn't the middle ages. She'd have worn armor made of nothing but tin cans.

But no, being a girl, she'd probably be expected to wait inside a stone castle and stitch a tapestry celebrating the glorious men. For a moment, Margo wondered what the women in her family had actually done over the years. Somehow she didn't think she could be the only female St. George who wanted to do more than needlework.

She scowled and peered up at the roiling sky. No way she would sit back and let other people decide her life for her. She began jogging in the direction of the cliffs, slipping easily into the steady pace of an experienced runner. With pleasure, Margo felt her trained muscles stretch and flex at her command, despite their earlier workout.

She was only breathing a little harder than she liked when she reached her destination. Just as Uncle Daniel had described, the spot was marked by a boulder resting on the edge of the bluff. The cliffside here was steep, crenellated with old stone that folded and cracked in on itself like wrapping paper that had been bunched into a drawer. Farther up the shore, close to the Medway house, the bluff had a lower, gentler grade with stairs leading down to the beach. But here, the waves dashed themselves against the rocks, and the narrow strip of sand lay hidden by the surge.

For a few moments, Margo paced the top of the cliff, looking for a way down. Nothing obvious. She lay flat on the rank weeds, head over the stone lip trying to get a better view of a small ledge below.

Possible – if the foothold didn't mask an eroded crumble of loose stone that would collapse under her weight.

But she had to know. Had to try.

Easing over the edge, fingers clutching for a hold on the wet grass, Margo slid down. Her feet settled on the ledge, felt the firm rock below her toes. She released a long, slow breath and carefully let go of the tough plants above. A convenient tree root looped out of a crack in the rock and then back in, giving her a sturdy handhold. Clutching this, Margo looked around.

The tiny ledge sloped down and widened under an overhang of rock...a path. It was a path, invisible from above, completely unnoticeable even from the sea.

"Thank you, Dad," Margo murmured.

Inching along the treacherously narrow trail, she slowly made her way downward. The track slipped into shadow, seeming to disappear. But no, it snaked between the folds of rock, sliding finally into an apparent crack.

Wishing she had brought a flashlight, breathing hard from mingled exhaustion and fear, Margo slipped in between the pressing stones. What if she got stuck? No one would ever find her. No one would ever hear her cries for help over the crashing surf below.

The crack between the rocks seemed to breathe as cool air sloughed from the depths.

Cold.

Silent.

A tomb.

Terror paralyzed her. Her heart hammered and sweat dripped down her back. This was too much. Who cared about the Medways or her glorious heritage?

Margo blinked rapidly and swallowed. If she gave up, what then? What else did she have in her second-rate life?

"I...I am a St. George," she forced through numbed lips. Using every scrap of will, she made her feet and legs shuffle on. Ignored the sea pounding below, ignored the slimy feel of sweating rock and then...she was through.

The rock opened wide, revealing a cave. Panting, Margo steadied herself against the clammy wall and felt ahead with her toes. The rough tumble of stones became steps under her feet. To her left and down several feet, waves poured through a much wider crack in the rock. Dim light shone through, despite the storm outside.

She had made it.

Margo stared around her. The uneven walls of the cavern rose larger than her house, high ceilinged from eons of rainwater eroding from above and ocean waves pounding from below. She could see the high water marks where years of tides had flowed in and out. The wild storm beating outside the cave was tamed by the slant and cleft in the rocks.

A perfect hiding place.

Her breath caught. There in the shadows. The long, beautiful shape of a small sailboat.

Feeling like she had entered a sacred place, Margo walked slowly forward. The sailboat her father had built. Resting in a cradle, waiting all these years for her.

"Thanks, Dad," she whispered once again.

Tired as she was, Margo began inspecting the craft. Her mother had been right – her father was careful. The masts, lines, and sails had all been wrapped in canvas against the elements and lay waiting to be refitted into their proper places. She guessed the unchanging temperature of the cave had allowed the years to pass without the damage of uncertain weather. No mice or insects would venture into this place to gnaw or nest.

The boat was simple. Open decks with only a small hold below where a person could store food or even curl up to sleep. This wasn't a craft intended for long voyages, Margo saw with a pang of worry. Would it be enough to get Sibby and her mom to safety?

Thrusting the fear away, Margo set herself to methodically prepare the boat for use. First she unwound the canvas swathes and spent long minutes examining the hull, even crawling underneath to ensure nothing had warped or split. Perfect. Every part of the boat was perfect.

Margo ran her hand along the side, taking deep pleasure in the smooth surface. Then, unsure of the height of the cave's entrance, she laid the mast and spar lengthwise along the boat and lashed them down. Carefully she tied whatever lines could be installed now, and put the rest inside where they could be easily reached.

Then cautiously releasing the ropes, Margo leaned her shoulder into the hull and pushed the boat from its cradle, down the ramp, and into the water.

For a moment the sailboat bobbed like an uncertain water creature finally released back to the sea. Then it floated calmly, ready.

With a sob, Margo realized that her father's legacy to her was seaworthy. She would be able to save her family from the fury of the dragons.

Mooring the boat carefully, she took the high and low tide marks into account. If the ocean calmed, she would be able to sail out of the cavern at high tide. If the storm continued to rage over the water, Margo didn't think her seamanship was good enough to keep the boat from breaking on the rocks. Regretfully, she patted the wooden hull and simply stood, savoring its beauty in the dimming half-light. Then resolutely, she turned from the boat and began the difficult climb back to the top of the cliff.

The sky darkened as heavy clouds obscured the horizon. Rain plastered her hair to her head and Margo shook with cold and exhaustion. Not that far off, she saw the warm lights of the Medway house.

They'd be sorry, she thought bitterly. Not long now before Margo St. George made them and all their kind pay for what they'd done to her family. She would get her mom and sister to safety – before her brother and uncle brought the fury of the dragons on them all – but they had to pay.

Slowly, as though drawn by a cord, she approached the house. Through the small windows, she saw Dr. Medway sitting at a desk with a stack of books around him. In another window, Jacob leaned wearily against a wall. And Addie – her enemy – paced back and forth in front of her twin.

Hatred blazed inside her and Margo clenched her fists. Should she lure Addie outside and try to defeat her? For a satisfying moment, she replayed the fight they had had by the water. No question, Margo was a better fighter. A surge of pride straightened her shoulders. Yeah, she could totally take Addie Medway.

But then what?

In sudden horror, Margo realized that defeating the other girl meant nothing. She would have to kill her classmate. No matter how she appeared, Addie Medway was a dragon. And that was what the St. Georges did – they killed dragons.

Bile rose in Margo's stomach. How could she think of murdering the other girl, no matter what she was?

What kind of monster had she turned into, that she would even think like that?

"I have to get away," she mumbled. Shock at the realization of what her glorious heritage had become, made her sick. Spun through her mind. Ate at her heart.

But she had seen Addie begin to change before her eyes. Had seen her twin tackle her to stop the transformation. Jacob knew what his sister was. Uncle Daniel would want them all dead. It's what the St. Georges did. It's what they had always done – wiped the dragon scourge from the earth.

Irresolute, Margo stood swaying slightly in the gusting storm. Eyes closed, she played out scenario after scenario. In every one, just like Sibby's drawings, blood smeared the ground.

Whose blood?

Who was going to die?

Sick with fear, Margo opened her eyes and looked around. This was the spot. The torn up grass, the blood on the stones dripping down the steps onto the beach....

She blinked and the vision cleared. Only water sluiced over the ground and steps – just an ocean storm.

When would all this happen?

"Hey, M..margo," Jacob's voice penetrated her ghastly visions. "T..trespassing again?"

Margo spun around to face him. Even in her frantic state she saw he looked white and exhausted, that he leaned heavily on his crutches. The wind ruffled his hair, blowing it up and around like the leaves on the gaunt trees that leaned away from the storm.

"You have to leave." The warning broke from her. "My uncle and brother...our family are dragon slayers...."

Even in the half-dark, she saw his lips whiten, but he straightened up as much as he could.

"T..trying to scare m..me?" His voice challenged her.

Margo laughed, half hysterical. "Yes...you need to be scared. My brother and uncle will hunt you now. My sister sees things before they happen. She saw blood...she saw...."

She couldn't say more. Choking, Margo spun on her heel and began running, back toward her home. Trying desperately to run back to the life when the St. George heritage was a lot of big talk.

Back to when the Medways were nothing more than classmates who rubbed her the wrong way.

Back to normal.

But normal had disappeared forever when she had seen Addie transform into a dragon.

When Margo had been transformed into the last of the St. George warriors.

TWENTY

WE HAVE TO GET AWAY!

JACOB

"I'm not scared," Addie said defiantly. "And I'm not running away from the stupid St. George bullies."

Jacob bit back the words he wanted to shout, clenched his fists to stop himself from trying to grab his sister and shake her. "Th..those are the b..bullies who almost killed M..mom!"

He hated his stammer. Hated that his weak body wouldn't allow him to take on the St. Georges himself. "D..dad?" He turned desperately to their father.

"It's not possible," their father said. "You are children...even these zealots wouldn't hurt children."

"Wh..why not?" Jacob demanded. "Y..you think they're th..thinking?"

"I could call the police," Dr. Medway said doubtfully.

"Great plan, Dad," Addie said scornfully. "*Hello officer…those crazy St. Georges think my children are dragons. They're threatening us. Well, yes, my daughter actually is a dragon, but they are harassing us!*" Addie snorted. "I'm sure you can pull that one off, Dad."

Dr. Medway sank down onto a kitchen chair. "You're right, of course."

Jacob wanted to punch something in frustration. "S..so what are w..we going to do? Margo s..said there would be b..blood."

He couldn't explain how her insane words brought a vision of destruction to his mind.

Vivid.

Horrifying.

Real.

He felt as if the blood pounding through his veins was heightening his awareness of his family's terrifying danger. He had to stop what was coming. Had to get his family away before it was too late.

"I'll think about all this," their father said helplessly. "I'll come up with a plan." He forced a smile to his face. "It's really too late to do anything tonight."

Jacob swung away and stood facing a window, trying to peer through the reflected light into the night beyond. How long before the dragon hunters came? How could his family get away? Despite not having a license, Jacob wondered for a moment if he could manage to drive away. But Addie was set on a fight. And their father wouldn't let go of the obsessive hope that their mother would come back to them.

Think! He commanded himself.

Outside, the storm howled in growing intensity. Wind rocked the trees and rain sleeted sideways, hammering against the house. Jacob felt his own heart hammering in response, its beat synchronizing with the elements. He laid his palms flat against the cold panes and leaned forward until his forehead touched the glass. Outside the world screamed its fury. Inside his head, the screaming grew ever wilder.

He had to do something. Anything. He had to have a plan.

Turning around he watched his father pick through another shelf of books. In her room upstairs, Addie had turned up the volume of her playlist until the music echoed the buffeting storm.

With a hiss of frustration, Jacob made his way to his own room, picked up his backpack and dumped out the contents. Notebooks, texts, pens and pencils scattered across the floor. Deliberately he began to move through the house to refill the pack. A rain poncho from the hall closet. First aid kit from the bathroom. Camping knife from the garage. Granola bars and water from the kitchen.

When the bag had been crammed full and lashed shut, he turned to see his sister watching.

"W..we're going to have to r..run," he told her.

Her eyes were stormy, but after a moment, she nodded curtly. "Do you think you can actually make Dad move," she demanded, "or are we going to leave him here?"

Jacob sat wearily on a stool. "We h..have to convince him."

"Good luck with that." Addie plunked down on the stool beside him. "He does this whole intelligent, reasonable thing, but you know he's actually crazy." She shoulder bumped her brother. "Don't ever forget, he married a dragon. He left sanity behind a long, long time ago."

They started laughing. Giggles rising to hysterical shrieks. Jacob slid off the stool, grasped at the counter and sank to the floor. Addie tried to catch him, stumbled and landed beside him. And still they laughed. When finally tears ran down their cheeks and they gasped for breath, they gave it up. Shakily,

Addie pulled her brother to his feet, and still snorting, Jacob still clutching the backpack, they stumbled off to bed.

"Tomorrow, bro," Addie said. "We'll make Dad face reality somehow."

Ten minutes later, as Jacob collapsed on his bed exhausted, his eyes fell on the backpack.

Pitiful.

The best he could do.

Outside, the storm raged on.

TWENTY-ONE

THE BLOOD ISN'T HERE

MARGO

Margo barely remembered getting home. As she forced herself to half-jog, half-stumble along the gravel road, the night became a nightmare of wind and sleeting rain. She had to lean into it, fight her way down the wet road, battle her way through the elements that had no mercy on anyone caught in the storm.

Unaccustomed lights lit up her house. Even as she slid in the door, she could hear her uncle's rasping voice rising and falling and Ryan's loud bragging to his friends on his phone. From somewhere upstairs, her mother shrilled at them to let her sleep, but as usual, they ignored her.

Margo knew she should go into the kitchen and face them, but she was too tired, could hardly hold her head up any longer. Instead she wearily trudged up the stairs to her room, and even more wearily mounted the ladder to the top bunk. Too exhausted to change into pajamas. Too tired to care.

Dawn had barely lightened the room, when Sibby climbed the ladder and poked her.

"Now!" her sister whispered. "We have to go now."

Margo awoke instantly, reached out and gently gripped her sister's arm. Sibby stood on the ladder rungs swaying forward and back, her face an emotionless mask.

"We have to go now," she repeated. "It's time."

"Okay, Sibby," Margo managed to mutter thickly. "Whatever you say."

Sibby climbed back down the ladder, and Margo sat up, rubbing sleep from her scratchy eyes. Her clothes had mostly dried during the night, but even to her own nose, she smelled awful. Sweat, wet, and dirt. Her sister was fully dressed and had a backpack on her shoulders.

"Hurry," Sibby urged, looking up at her. "The dragons are angry. The picture is going to happen soon."

Margo swung herself out of the bunk, not bothering with the ladder. Fully awake now, she felt as though firecrackers exploded in her brain, overlaying the memory of Sibby's drawing – the one where blood pooled in the grass and dripped on the beach steps.

"We have to get Mom," Margo told her.

Sibby frowned but said nothing when Margo raced into her mom's room.

"Mom!" Margo shook her mother. "We have to go. Ryan and Uncle Daniel are going to shoot someone."

"Yeah, right," her mother mumbled. She opened her eyes a fraction. "I don't care if the house falls down. I'm not getting out of bed." Her eyes drifted shut again.

"*Mom!*" Margo shook her again. Her mother muttered something incoherent and rolled away, turning her back to her.

Margo stood helplessly for a moment until Sibby slid into the room and took her hand. "We have to go. The blood isn't here."

Margo hesitated, breathing hard – her mother wasn't going to move. Sibby tugged urgently. Her sister had never insisted before.

The blood isn't here....

Margo nodded curtly. "I found my dad's boat. I'll get you away, Sibby."

The two girls ran down the stairs. Ryan sprawled across the sofa, asleep, a shotgun dangling loosely from his hand. Margo shivered. There was no sign of Uncle Daniel.

"He's watching," Sibby whispered. "But they aren't where he watches. They're coming."

"Then we'd better move it," Margo replied softly.

They eased out the door and set off down the road paralleling the coast. Margo's muscles protested, but she set as fast a pace as she could. Sibby determinedly ran beside her. Margo took the backpack and slung it onto her own shoulders, then held her sister's hand tightly as though to prevent her from being tossed into the air by the gusting winds.

They left the road and pushed through wet weeds and scrub to the section of bluff that hid the path down to the cavern. Sibby crouched and peered over the edge as Margo slid down to the trail. She held up her hand to steady her sister, but Sibby didn't seem to need help. She was more agile than Margo had ever expected and utterly unafraid of the drop to the rocks and waves below.

From their perch on the ledge, Margo let her sister go along the path first, ready to catch her if she slipped, but Sibby moved lightly, fearless and surefooted, hesitating only a fraction of a second before plunging into the shadowy rock cleft leading downward. The sound of slapping waves and smell of dank salty air hit Margo's senses. Resolutely she pushed back any fear that was trying to build in her brain. She was a warrior. She didn't feel fear – and if she did, she would never let it stop her.

When they reached the cavern where the boat waited, Sibby rooted through the pack on Margo's shoulders, pulled out a strong flashlight, and aimed it at the bobbing craft.

"Hurry," she commanded. She shone the light at the cave entrance where water marks glistened on the stone walls. With a shock, Margo realized the tide had turned and before long, the water would be too low to sail from the cavern.

Without speaking, she jumped onto the boat and moving like a cat, darted over the deck ensuring all the lines were properly fastened and the sail and mast were ready to hoist as soon as they cleared the rock walls. When she checked below the deck, she saw with intense satisfaction that no water had leaked into the hold.

"You did it right, Dad," she murmured.

When all was ready, she turned to her sister who had waited quietly, simply shining the light where it was needed. Margo held out a steadying hand and Sibby clambered down. Her sister crouched in the front of the boat, looking like a figurehead adorning the prow.

Margo smiled and loosed the boat from its moorings.

Using the oars, Margo stroked them slowly forward, sometimes using pressure on the sweating walls to get them around the sharp bends in the channel. Water lapped and swirled around them, tugging, pushing, pulling. There was barely enough space to pass – twice the hull scraped against rock. But hoping there was no damage, she eased them through the passage.

In the front, Sibby barely moved.

The sweating walls slid by. The closer they got to open sea, the rougher the surging water. While keeping the sailboat from crashing into the walls, Margo tried to feel the rhythm of the water. Ahead, light gleamed, beckoning, while the slap of waves churning against rocks filled her ears. The boat lurched beneath their feet, eddying again toward the upthrust stones. When one huge swell rushed inwards, Margo desperately drove them up and over the crest, rowing forward with every ounce of strength she had. They burst from the tunnel into open water, soaked by spray, nearly blinded by glistening sun. The storm clouds were fast disappearing, leaving only wind behind.

Laughing in triumph, Margo stroked hard until their craft dipped and danced on the ocean, well away from the rocky bluffs. The pitching waves under the boards made her feel utterly alive. Rapidly, she fitted the masts and sails, ready to steer the craft south, as far from the dragons as she could get.

"No." Sibby suddenly stood, pointing north.

"Sit down," Margo yelled.

But Sibby ignored her and faced resolutely up the coast, toward the Medway's house. Toward the site of her drawings. Toward the dripping blood.

"No, Sibby," Margo pleaded. "We have to get away."

But her sister simply stared north, her finger pointing unwaveringly up the coast toward the Medway's house, towards destruction.

"I have to keep you safe," Margo protested. She gripped the rudder, wanting desperately to slew the boat around, to sail south to safety.

"It's time for the last warrior to fight." Sibby's voice barely rose above the swash of the waves. "Margo, it's time for you to fight the dragons."

TWENTY-TWO

YOU'LL PAY
JACOB

When Jacob opened his eyes in the morning, the room lay in grey darkness. Rain no longer battered the roof, but clouds overshadowed the sky. He longed to stay where he was, slip back into a cocoon of sleep, but anger and fear had begun their insistent hammering in his mind. Wearily, he forced himself to get out of bed and struggle into his clothes. There was no sound of anyone else moving around the house.

He slung the backpack over his shoulder and left his room. Addie's door was shut – still asleep he guessed. For a moment, he paused and listened. No muttering sounds or cries, so for once her sleep was peaceful. His father's bedroom door stood open, sheets and blankets rumpled, but surprisingly there was no sign of his dad. Dr. Medway wasn't in the kitchen or his study either. Anxiously, Jacob dropped the pack on a chair and went out the back door. The clouds were clearing but the gusts were fierce, adding to his struggle as he made his way through the tangled overgrowth.

His father stood on the edge of the bluff, arms hanging limply at his sides as he stared out over the ocean.

"It was here," his dad said. "That's why I bought this house. This is where I found your mother."

Jacob stared at his father. Disbelief warred with lashing fury. "You brought us to the place where the crazies tried to murder her?" he shouted. "You're completely insane! And now they're going to try and kill Addie. What kind of father are you?"

His father stepped back as though he had been punched, then turned to Jacob, eyes wide. "Not...not a sensible one. I'm sorry Jacob. I'm sorry."

"L..like that's going to h..help!" Jacob tried to whack his dad with the crutch. Didn't care that there was moisture dripping down his father's face.

His father stared and then abruptly straightened. "I haven't been thinking. Not thinking at all. We'll leave today...this morning. Nothing is worth putting you or your sister in danger."

"A..about t..time," Jacob snarled, but relief edged through him. If his father would finally take over, make plans, drive the truck...maybe they could make it. Maybe they could escape this nightmare.

"I..I'll get Addie," he said.

Turning back toward the house, he froze. Rough motors sounded on the gravel road. Squealing tires. Savage shouting.

And a shotgun blast.

Two old pick-ups, loaded with jeering boys and men, spun into the driveway blocking their truck.

Unable to move, Jacob watched as Ryan St. George, brandishing a gun, leapt nimbly out of one of the trucks. His gang of bullies poured out of the cabs and backs of the vehicles. Ryan turned and used his great muscles to lift a man in a wheelchair from the truck bed and set him down on the driveway.

"You're finished," the man yelled. His eyes were wide and spittle flew from his mouth as he shook his fist. "You worms ain't gonna get away now!"

"Don't even try to run, you spaz," Ryan threatened loudly. "We got you covered. Now where's that witch of a sister? We're gonna get her good!"

He cocked his gun and swung it around. The other boys shouted and jeered, waving their firearms and baseball bats.

"No, wait!" Dr. Medway called. He strode toward Ryan, arms wide, placating. "This makes no sense! We need to talk!"

"This is the only talkin' we do," shrieked the man. "You killed my brother! You did this to me!" He grabbed Ryan's gun from his hands, aimed it at Jacob's dad, and with a howl of hatred, pulled the trigger.

"No!" Jacob screamed.

The explosion reverberated through the air. His father staggered back and then, with a queer bubbling gasp, crumpled to the ground.

"Dad!" Jacob yelled. Rushing, stumbling, Jacob made it to his father and, dropping his crutches, fell to his knees. Behind him, the sudden silence slowly gave way to taunts and threats, an ugly chorus tossed on the gusting wind.

"Dad," Jacob pleaded. His father looked up at him, eyes wide in bewilderment, but then his lids fluttered and closed.

Frantic, Jacob tried to shake his dad back to consciousness, but it was useless. Blood seeped everywhere, over his father's clothes, on his own desperate hands, into the grass.

Tears streaming down his face, Jacob stared at the hunters. Anger began building in him.

"You'll p..pay for this!" He shouted the promise. "You'll pay."

TWENTY-THREE

THE ENEMY COMES

ADDIE

The voices wouldn't leave her alone. Addie had been soaring like an eagle across the wind currents, over the stark coastline, uplifted by the elements. And then the voices began to harry her like angry crows, diving, pecking, slicing.

She screamed like an angry eagle too, but it did no good. The shrieking voices pecked at her, demanding she leave the skies, return to the ground. Addie swooped and veered, banked and turned until one voice stood out from the rest.

"*Mom?*"

And she was tumbling then, falling, plummeting down into her human self. Her mother's voice rose above the vicious others.

Addie plunged awake. Sat straight up in her bed. Clapped her silver-tipped hands to her head and slowly, sobbing, forced all the ghastly dragon voices back, cleared her thoughts....

"*Adara...*" Her mother's call had become a desperate whisper, tossed on winds. "*Darling girl...your father...they've come. Save your father...save your brother.*"

"Mom!" Addie's voice broke. Her hands reached into the air as if she could grasp the mother who belonged to the words.

"*They broke my wings....*" Despair wailed through the air. "*Save them, Addie....*"

"Mom!" A rising cry of her own anguish tore from Addie's throat, but the dragon voices blocked her, their snarls echoing even in her human mind.

"No!" she shouted. Dragon rage was building in her, and then – a gunshot.

Addie felt and heard her brother's scream.

"*Jacob!*" She struggled from the bed and ran from her room, through the house. As she tore out the kitchen door, she saw the trucks, heard the roars from the hunters. Saw her father sprawled in the grass. Her brother, crutches cast aside, bent over their father's body as though to protect him.

The hunters almost danced their savagery, guns and weapons held high as they shouted and congratulated each other, yowled their triumph over the unarmed man. Surrendered themselves to blood lust.

In the center of their circle, a man in a wheelchair, thrust his fist in the air, and yelled.

"We ain't got 'em all, boys!" His face contorted like a madman. "We still got more to kill!"

A roar of hatred exploded from Addie's throat. She sprang toward them, felt the power of her heritage erupt into her veins. Silver mist filled her vision and she leapt into the air, wings beating, silver claws extended.

Her enemies weren't ready.

Fangs dripping, silver lips drawn back in a hideous snarl, Addie grabbed guns from their weakened grasps and hurled the weapons over the cliff into the water. Boys squealed and scrambled for their trucks, holding arms over their heads as Addie, wild with rage, raked them with her talons. When she had harried the weaklings away, she turned back, hate consuming her heart, to the cause of all her pain.

Ryan had grabbed a gun and pointed it at her.

Claws extended, Addie dove toward him. As Ryan pulled the trigger, Jacob launched himself onto the bully, driving the aim off target.

"Get off!" Ryan cursed and backhanded Jacob, sending him tumbling onto the rocky ground.

But it was enough. The bullet whizzed past Addie, not touching her. Screaming in fury, she dove at Ryan. He swung the stock of his gun like a baseball bat, into the bones that supported the gossamer of her silver wings.

Crack! Addie screamed, faltered in pain, and clawed the air.

Deep in her mind, the snarling dragons fought for a new hold on her. The cracked old voice drove them on. Desperate, Addie flew higher, away from the St. Georges, shaking her head, trying to fight off the biting, thrusting attack of the wild dragons. One cruel, ancient voice drove all the others.

When she thought she couldn't fight any longer, a blaze of silver blue rose in front of her. Her mother. Audra struggled into the battle, fighting, snapping back at the feral beasts. Addie felt her mother's defiant agony as the others turned on her. Tore at her maimed wings.

"*Go, Addie*," her mother cried.

And behind her mother's voice, she heard a different, distant chorus beginning. *Take our strength, daughter*, whispered in her thoughts. Somehow, these voices quieted the ones who hunted her.

Addie felt a stream of ancient magic reaching toward her. First a trickle, then finally a torrent of the old knowledge...and its first love of humankind. With it came new strength. Despite her near-crippled limb, Addie backwinged into the sky. Spent bullets glanced harmlessly off her skin. Below, the St. Georges screamed and cursed.

And her twin, Jacob, sprawled half-conscious in the rank weeds.

Her father lay bleeding beside him.

"*Bring him to me*," her mother whispered. "*If we combine our strength, we can save our family.*"

Below, Ryan picked up a bat and advanced on Jacob.

"No!" Addie shrieked and dove toward him. The man in the wheel chair laughed like a madman and raised a gun.

Addie swooped down, knocking him from the chair, grazing his shoulder with her talons until the blood flowed. He clawed at the air as his wheelchair tipped over, spilling him onto the ground. Wild with rage, Addie flew at Ryan.

He raised the bat to strike her, but then suddenly stumbled. Jacob, blood streaming down his cheek had managed to thrust his crutch between Ryan's legs.

When the bully went down, Addie landed on his chest. Ryan wailed and tried to beat at her. Addie sank down to her human self and kneeled astride him.

"No," he cried. "I'll kill you. I'll hunt you... don't hurt me!"

"You're pathetic, Ryan St. George," she hissed. "Run, before I destroy you!"

She sat back and watched as Ryan scrambled to his feet and ran for the road. His friends had taken the trucks.

"Ryan!" the man from the wheelchair croaked after him, but his nephew didn't stop.

Addie ignored the crippled man scrabbling at the grass, and turned to her brother who was sitting up and frantically keying numbers into his cell phone.

"There's been an accident," her brother was shouting into the phone. "An attack...I think my father's dying..."

Addie raced to her father. She knelt beside him and tried to stop the blood. But she couldn't. The gaping wound in his shoulder still bled and the grass was wet with his blood.

"Daddy," she lifted his head into her arms.

"*Bring him, Addie,*" her mother's voice pleaded in her mind. "*Before it's too late....*"

"I...I think I may be done for..." her father

whispered. "I believe...losing so much blood... is often fatal..."

Fighting back sobs, Addie looked for help. Any help. Her arm throbbed where her wing had been struck.

"*Bring him, Addie,*" her mother begged.

"I can't," Addie cried. How could she carry her father? But she had to try somehow. And she couldn't leave Jacob. The crazy man was still here. Ryan might come back...

She was overwhelmed with the disaster around her. And then another figure ran up from the beach – *Margo St. George.*

She had no hope now. Her enemy had come.

TWENTY-FOUR

TIME FOR YOU TO DIE

JACOB

Jacob shouted their address to the emergency services on his phone. There was blood everywhere. He had to think...had to decide what to do to save his family. Addie cradled their unconscious father in her lap. His dad's shirt was thick with blood.

"First aid...f..first aid," Jacob muttered to himself. He had to stop the bleeding. But how?

From the corner of his eye, Jacob saw the man in the wheelchair dragging himself across the ground, reaching for a gun. Jacob moved faster. Viciously, he used his crutch to whack the rifle away, sending it spinning over the bluff. The man collapsed onto the ground sobbing and cursing.

"I hope you die!" Jacob screamed.

He wanted to attack his enemy but instead,

he yanked his mind back to the crisis in front of him.

"No!" Addie yelled.

Jacob twisted around. Margo St. George ran lightly up the steps from the beach, then stopped, staring at the mayhem, her face whitening.

"*Margo!*" the man yelled, his voice thick and mad. "Kill them, Margo! Kill these vermin!"

Jacob stumbled over to stand in front of his family. How could he protect them from this new onslaught? What could he do? Rage was building in him in a way he had never felt before.

Margo's eyes strayed over to Jacob's dad and her expression hardened.

"I'll help you," she said brusquely. "We have to stop the bleeding. And then we have to get away. My brother and his stupid gang may come back."

Addie seemed unable to move, so Jacob drove himself hard to get into the house. He grabbed the backpack and a stack of clean dish towels from the kitchen, and balancing precariously, rushed back out. Margo was on her knees beside Addie.

Jacob dropped to the ground beside them. Addie rooted in his pack for antiseptic while

Margo ripped open their dad's shirt. Once Addie had poured the cleanser over their dad's chest, Margo folded the towels into a pad, and bound them tightly over the wound. Her face shone with perspiration.

"This is your fault, Margo!" Addie accused.

Margo shook her head. "No! No, I didn't...." She looked up suddenly as the growl of an engine sounded in the distance. "We have to get away."

"Margo..." her uncle whined.

"You! You crazy old man," Margo said fiercely. "Uncle Daniel, I don't want to ever speak to you again!" Breathing hard, she turned to Jacob. "If Addie and I carry your dad, can you make it to the beach? I have a boat."

"Yes," Jacob said. He didn't know if he could make it. His arms were shaking and his head was pounding with the aftermath of his fury. But if he had to slide down on his head, he wouldn't slow down the girls as they tried to save his father.

Addie's arm clearly showed her injury as she tried to hoist her dad.

"I'll take his head," Margo told her.

Addie nodded and switched places, lifting her father's legs as Margo gently lifted his shoulders. Jacob stood motionless, listening to the truck getting nearer and nearer. No sirens yet. How long before the police came and stopped this? And his father...?

Somehow, Margo and Addie managed to get their father down the steep steps. Jacob closed his ears to his parent's groans and concentrated on getting himself down to the shore below. Twice his crutch slipped but he managed to stay upright.

A small sailboat had been pulled onto the beach. A girl of about eleven, her form highlighted by a slash of brilliant orange from a life jacket, stood silently in the prow, watching them.

Addie and Margo eased Dr. Medway into the boat as gently as they could. He groaned again and slid more deeply into unconsciousness.

"Sibby...my sister...says we have to find the dragons." Margo's wide gaze swept between the twins' faces.

"The d..dragons," Jacob said. "Yes! Our mother c..can heal our father."

"If the others don't kill us first," Addie muttered. She crouched down beside their dad, holding his hand.

"We won't l..let them," Jacob said. He looked up at Margo. "Dragons h..have the power to heal. It's Dad's only ch..chance."

"Fantastic," Margo muttered. "Addie's report is real. And I'm an idiot."

Jacob froze. *Shouting. Yelling.* "We have to go!" Fear sharpened his voice.

Margo literally dragged him into the boat, then sprang back onto the beach and shoved the hull until the craft floated free on the water. She sloshed through the waves and climbed nimbly in, while Jacob stared up at the bluff. Terror and rage warred equally in him. How many minutes...seconds...before the hunters found them?

He barely noticed Margo's quick actions as she tossed life jackets to them, set the sail, and turned the prow out toward open ocean. Addie moved to crouch beside him. He could see the shimmer of silver as her dragon fury rose.

"I want to kill them," she hissed.

"No," Jacob shot back. "We have to g..get Dad away."

She nodded and the silver sheen lessened. He twisted around. Behind them, Margo's face was set and white, her freckles red blotches on her pale skin as she steered the craft into the waves. The wind had dropped to a stiff breeze, but Jacob was sure it took strength and skill to keep them on course. He bit his lip as Margo's brother, Ryan, and two of his friends suddenly appeared at the top of the bluff. They shouted and waved their guns, but maybe Addie's earlier attack had scared them into caution.

"Thank you for h..helping us," Jacob said stiffly to Margo. She nodded curtly, but didn't answer, her attention seemingly focused on her task. Only once did she look back over her shoulder at the hunters on the bluff.

"Sibby," she called suddenly. "Where to from here?"

The girl in the prow pointed at Jacob. "He has to talk to the dragons."

"No," Jacob protested. "I d..don't know how." He turned to his sister. "Addie," he said urgently, "can you call M..mom?"

His sister shook her head. "I can't. The dragon clan is searching for me. Their queen, the white one...she's still trying to kill me. What about you, Jacob? They don't know to hunt for you. You're family...even if you aren't a dragon. Mom should be able to hear you."

Jacob stared. Behind them, Ryan's threats carried across the wind. A bullet whizzed by and splashed into the waves.

"Do something fast," Margo yelled. "Or your dad is dead. I don't know where to go!"

Panicked, Jacob looked from one to the other. Sibby turned her head to gaze at him, her face curiously blank. "Call your mother."

Wanting to yell with the hopelessness that washed over him, Jacob stared down at the deck. Their father's blood mixed with the spray, running in red streaks over the boards.

"I'll t..try," Jacob snapped.

Not knowing what else to do, he closed his eyes and frantically tried to picture his mom. He could see her so clearly, laughing and playing with them. He felt an outpouring of love...and then bitter loss.

Mom, he whispered across the void. *Mom, please, we need you.*

Another bullet zinged through the air. He heard it smack into the side of the hull, followed by Margo's muttered curses.

His eyes flew open again, as with a roar, Addie suddenly erupted into dragon form. She winged into the air, sun gleaming across her silver skin. He watched her scream her rage as she flew high and then dove at the men waving their guns. A volley of shots filled the air. Both hearing and feeling her shriek of pain, Jacob saw Addie backwing awkwardly, one leg held up against her body.

Instinctively, his mind shot out to her, supporting her. The hurt spasmed across his own weak leg and he would have keeled over had he not steadied himself against the mast. With a deep breath, he closed his eyes and willed strength to his sister. He felt her slow wingbeats, the pain that tore through her, then dizziness and terror as the hunting dragons found her and zeroed in on her mind.

"No!" Jacob roared.

They would not harm his twin. The anger that had been simmering inside him erupted, exploded through his being. He stood up, barely aware of the glittering sapphire sheen that masked his mind and vision.

As Addie spun downward, shifting into her human form, Jacob sprang upward. Like fireworks that crackled in the night, his DNA awoke. Instinct driven, Jacob spread his vast wings and reached to catch his sister before she fell into the waves. With his new self fizzing in his mind, barely conscious that he was doing so, Jacob flew in easy circles to bring them both down gently onto the deck of the boat.

"*My son,*" whispered in his thoughts. "*You and your sister must come to me, to the clan.*"

"Mom?"

Suddenly, a cracked, manic voice pierced his mind. "*Come to us, half-blood,*" the old queen's voice hissed. "*It is time for you to die.*"

TWENTY-FIVE

THEY KNOW WE'RE COMING

ADDIE

Addie huddled on the floor of the sailboat. She couldn't think about her brother's transformation...not yet. The pain throbbing in her injured leg and arm made it hard to think at all. But she couldn't give into it, couldn't just sit there whimpering no matter how bad it was. Panting, she gingerly moved her arm. Her shoulder ached, sending a wave of nausea through her, but she could use her arm if she was careful.

"You're bleeding." Margo's flat voice pushed through the pain. "We need to bandage your leg."

Addie glanced at the girl's white, set face, and then down at her leg. The fabric of her jeans was scorched and wet with blood. The pain from the gunshot wound in her calf rippled up and through her body like fire. Like she was being burned with molten agony.

She steadied herself and using her good hand, pulled back the fabric. Her skin was torn, bleeding sluggishly, but there was no bullet hole – just a long, black-edged gash.

"I think I'm okay," she managed.

"Whatever." Margo jerked a thumb at Jacob, crouched in a tight ball to one side of the deck. "He has to find out how to get to the dragons or we're dead. Even my idiot brother will remember there are motorboats in town. I can't outrun a speedboat."

Addie took a hissing breath and, allowing just a little dragon strength loose, forced herself to stand, grateful that her leg didn't buckle under her. "Jacob!" She leaned over her twin. "Hey bro, are you okay?"

He raised his eyes to hers, still sapphire blue, still gleaming with dragon light. "I..I'm okay. A little sh..shook...a little surprised...." He forced a laugh. "Seems you're n..not the only dragon in the family."

She sank down beside him and bumped her good shoulder gently against his. "Cool..."

He nodded and straightened as fire lit his eyes. "I'm n..not crippled as a d..dragon. I c..can fly. I'm strong...I'm *strong!*"

"You always have been," Addie blinked her eyes rapidly. This was so not the time to get emotional. "I heard the crazy voice, the murdering one, threatening you. Do you think she has a bead on you?"

Her brother's cheeks whitened, but he shook his head. "Prob..ably not yet. Doesn't m..matter. We have to find the c..clan…fast."

They both looked at their father, lying unconscious on the deck. Addie watched Jacob draw a harsh breath and close his eyes. Like a faint, whispered echo, she could hear him questing for their mother, for the way to dragons' hidden caverns. But she knew already he couldn't communicate clearly. In their human skins, neither of them was powerful enough. Hidden in their humanity, the dragons couldn't find them; but the brother and sister couldn't find the dragons or their secrets either.

"You two better figure this out." Margo's voice broke in harshly. "Otherwise your father isn't going to make it." She glanced back at the bluff receding in the distance. "The idiots have left. They'll be along in a boat before long, so maybe none of us will make it."

"Fantastic," Addie snapped. "You must just love your family."

Margo's fingers whitened on the rudder. "Seems like your kin are trying to kill you, too," she snarled. "So I wouldn't get so snotty, Addie."

Addie snapped her mouth shut and felt the heat rush into her cheeks. She hated Margo! Hated especially that she was right.

But she and Jacob were both reluctant – make that *terrified* – to face the dragons again. For long moments, the twins leaned against each other and looked ahead up the coast.

"Well?" Margo demanded.

"Not yet," Addie snapped. "You don't know what it's like...what they're like. And Jacob has to get ready for it."

Margo said nothing, but returned to scanning the coastline ahead and behind. Addie tried to steady her breathing. Time stretched around them as they skirted miles of shoreline. Margo tended to the boat. Sibby sat motionless in the prow. Despite herself, despite her human form, Addie heard a growing murmur of dragon voices. Beside her, she felt Jacob tense. He heard them too.

"It's time to weave the strings together." Sibby's words floated gently in the breeze. She left the prow and kneeling, slipped her hand into Jacob's. "Find the dragons," she whispered. "Be the dragon now. Talk to the dragons."

Addie could have wept. "I can do it," she managed. "I'll draw them out."

“No,” Jacob said. “They aren’t h..hunting me...” He stood up awkwardly, grasping the side of the boat for support. For a moment he shut his eyes. When he opened them, they had fully changed to gleaming shards of sapphire. And then the sheen spread across his body. Addie caught her breath, and behind her, heard Margo’s gasp. Suddenly, Jacob leapt upwards, his body morphing into that of a dragon, shimmering and glorious against the cloudy sky.

Addie, still spellbound, watched as he circled above the boat, his surge of joy echoing within her. She wanted to join him. Wanted to soar above the waves and feel the wind lifting and carrying her upward. Instinctively, she reached out her arms, ready to leap in the air. A strong hand yanked her back to the boat’s deck, and she cried out at the sudden pain.

Margo gripped Addie’s sore arm tightly. “Not now,” she growled. “You’ll bring them on us before we find the caves. Out here, you and your brother can fly away, but Sibby and I are helpless. I won’t let them hurt my sister.”

Addie pulled back her arm, bringing her rational mind with it. Breathing hard, she looked down at her injured father and then over at the young girl sitting like a small statue. “You’re right,” she managed. “Sorry.”

Margo grunted and returned to the task of steering the boat. Addie tried not to notice that her once enemy's hands shook, that her face was as white as the crests on the waves. Instead, she concentrated on Jacob, trying to hear what his thoughts ferreted out, trying to pour whatever weak strength she had into him.

Suddenly he wheeled around and dropped until his feet neared the boat. The sails flapped wildly.

"No!" Addie yelled.

Too late. Human Jacob crashed down onto the deck. The craft rocked wildly, but Margo somehow held it steady.

"N..need more p..practice," he panted. He pushed himself upright and like Sibby, pointed north. "Th..that way. Lots of rocks in.. in the surf. Cave behind it. C..couple of miles." He paused, breathing hard. "The clan know we're c..coming."

Addie rubbed his shoulders as he hung his head. She knew what a return to human form felt like – as though overstretched senses were smothered in packaging foam. But as the heightened emotions that felt so glorious receded, their human minds began working again.

"If they know we're coming, it could be rough." She turned to Margo. "Do you and your sister want to pull ashore? No one should have to face them."

She saw her enemy's face harden. "I'm made for this," she said. "The last of the dragon slayers."

Addie wanted to hit her, wanted to take her anger out on the people who had ruined her family's life, but the dragon emotions had calmed. "What about Sibby?"

"I'm going to talk to them." The girl suddenly turned and smiled at them.

"No, Sibby!" Margo exclaimed.

"You can't talk to them," Addie told her. "They're savage. Completely wild. You don't know...." She stopped abruptly. In the distance, the whine of a motorboat slapping over waves was unmistakable.

"Too late," Margo said.

Addie looked back over the water. Rounding a bluff, a sleek speedboat crowded with a half a dozen shouting men, bounced over the surf. Margo's uncle held the wheel.

Fighting back the wave of panic, Addie turned to Margo. "So how fast can you make this thing go?"

TWENTY-SIX

DESTINY AND DOOM

MARGO

Raw fear clutched Margo – she knew better than anyone how insane her Uncle Daniel had become. How he would stop at nothing to get revenge. Even if it meant murder. Even if it meant his nieces drowning in the wild surf. And her brother, Ryan.... Margo's lip curled in disdain. Her brother had abandoned thinking a long time ago. Had surrendered himself to the easy thrill of power that came from bullying. If she and Sibby suffered, he'd just shrug it off.

Ironic that her best hope for saving herself and Sibby lay in helping, instead of hunting, the dragons.

"We have to fix the tapestry." Sibby looked back and smiled again.

Margo wondered bitterly if Sibby was as crazy as her uncle, just in a better way.

The wind whipping across the ocean had blown away the last of the storm clouds, but huge waves still rolled under the prow of the boat. Margo had not let on how hard she'd been fighting to keep control, to steer close to land, and still make speed. The dragon twins obviously knew nothing about sailing. Neither of them had even noticed how the gusts had fought with the over-stretched sails.

She should have reefed the sails, or gone further out. But she needed to stay close to shore in case the boat keeled over and they were all thrown into the ocean. Maybe the dragons wouldn't care, but Margo had been measuring distance, assessing how far she would have to swim to save Sibby and herself.

Dr. Medway probably wouldn't survive.

If she'd had any brains at all, she would have carried her sister ashore and left the dragons to their fate.

But she couldn't. Even if it hadn't been a death sentence for Dr. Medway, she couldn't save herself at the cost of the kids she had sat in class with. Shared barbs, taunts, and blows with. Bitterly, Margo realized that Addie's tongue and Jacob's toughness had earned her regard in ways her other friends never had. Like her, the twins knew what it meant to fight their way through life.

The wind gusted again, making the boat heel. Again she fought with the rudder and sails, impatiently pulled sopping hair from her eyes, forced her aching muscles to keep going. Glancing back, she saw the speed boat was gaining. Ahead, a barrier of rocks towered above the turbulent water.

"It's th..there." Jacob stood and pointed past the surf crashing over the upthrust stones, to a black crease in the face of the cliff. "Inside the c..crack."

"We'll break up on the rocks," Margo shouted.

"I could carry Sibby and Jacob could carry you," Addie shouted back. "But my dad..."

"No one gets left behind," Margo snarled. "I'll do it. I'll get us there."

"They're coming now," Sibby said. She stood up and pointed.

"I know...." Margo had been staring back at the boat closing on them, but as they neared the rocks, she looked ahead.

Like jeweled bats, the creatures erupted from a crack in the cliff. Sunlight glinted on silver, blue, and green wings. The dragons spiraled upward, nearly black against the sun, wide wings beating as they soared on the currents of air. One huge dragon, white as ice crystals, wheeled high and higher, flying above them all.

So deadly.

So beautiful.

Her destiny and her doom.

Margo stood transfixed, forgetting everything, as she watched the fearsome dance in the sky.

Slam!

Addie punched her in the shoulder. "The boat!" she screamed.

Rocks loomed ahead. Margo yanked the rudder; the boat heeled but miraculously didn't tip. On the deck ahead, a glow spread over Addie and her brother. An instant later, both morphed into dragons and leapt into the air. Jacob soared sapphire blue and powerful. Addie gleamed silver, but Margo could see she labored a bit as her wounds hampered her. Sibby stood, arms held aloft as though waiting for one of the great beasts to lift her up from the plunging craft. High above, the crystal white dragon screamed the hunt.

A bullet whined past and embedded itself in the wooden deck. Margo yanked her eyes from the dragons, cursed long and hard, and struggling for breath as she fought with wind and waves, wished she could transform into a dragon herself, and drive her brother and uncle into the ocean.

A volley of shells hit the water. Good thing Ryan and his stupid friends were too lazy to ever have learned to shoot properly. But they might get lucky.

Forcing herself to ignore the dragons circling above, Margo made her decision. With a twist of the rudder, she sent the boat directly toward the rocks. Between the upthrust stones and cliff, a narrow passage offered a chance. She didn't know if she had the skill needed to navigate it, but for now it was her only hope.

Above, screams of rage echoed from the cliffs. Behind her the whine of the motorboat almost drowned out the shouts of the boys and the curses of her uncle. She didn't dare look either back or up, didn't dare watch what was happening. She had to focus every fiber of her being on the swirling water and deadly rocks.

The sailboat rose on a wave and smashed sideways against a tooth of stone. Margo cried out as she saw Sibby lurch.

"Sit down," she screamed.

But her sister stood up again, ignoring the wild wash of spray and the looming rocks. Again holding her arms aloft.

"Sibby," Margo begged. "Sibby, sit down."

On the deck before her, Dr. Medway groaned and stirred. Behind her, she could hear the feral howls of her brother and uncle, rising even above the roars of the dragons.

Ahead the rocks were too close together, the surf too wild. Margo let go of the rudder and ran forward to grab her sister. Holding the squirming girl in one arm, she reached back and clutched a fistful of Dr. Medway's shirt.

All her training, all her stupid dreams....

The boat rose on a wave, swung sideways, and with a horrifying crunch smashed into the rocks. The deck heaved beneath them and the craft shattered. The mast keeled over slowly and Margo's feet skidded on the tilting, broken deck.

Then bitter cold water swallowed her, knocking the breath from her body.

But she would hold on. She would hold on to Sibby and the injured man until there was nothing left within her.

She had to hold on.

Gripping with all her strength, trying to kick to the surface, waves and tides pulled Margo under; water closed over their heads.

But she held on....

TWENTY-SEVEN

KILL THEM!
JACOB

Jacob beat his wings and screamed defiance. He was strong! He was powerful! And he would never give this up.

Talons extended, he dove down, raking the skin of a small green dragon. The creature screamed and convulsed...then its pain suddenly reverberated in Jacob's awareness. Jacob shook his head, trying to clear his mind. The dragon beneath him was flapping its wings, losing control, spiraling into the ocean.

With a cry of agony, Jacob dove down, claws extended – this time to save, not destroy. Addie, wings beating unevenly from her own injuries, winged beside him. In the back of his mind, in the back of both of their minds, Jacob heard the mad screaming of the ancient white dragon, pounding, biting, trying to control them.

Again, Jacob shook his head. At he forced the savage howls from his mind, his claws fastened on a wing of the green dragon. Addie grabbed the other. Together, they backwinged, lifted the thrashing creature from the surging ocean. Dimly Jacob realized this dragon was very young, a hatchling...one of the last hatchlings...

He didn't think he could hold on much longer, couldn't support the weight. But then one of the silver dragons, bugling rage, swept underneath them, cradling the green dragon on her back. Beating her massive wings, she made for the crack in the cliff.

Flushed with relief, Jacob flew high.

The other dragons circled above. The cracked voice pierced his thoughts again, but Jacob thrust them from his mind. He wouldn't listen! Wouldn't let his mind become crippled the way his body had been crippled.

He was free, free for the first time in his life and nothing would take that from him.

"*Jacob!*" Addie screamed.

Bewildered, he looked at her, and then down at the water. The sailboat had crashed into rocks, foundered, was sinking. A red life jacket bobbed in the waves.

"*Dad!*" Jacob dove downwards, hunting in the water. Panic roiled in him...how could he have forgotten? How could the wild freedom of one side of his heritage make him forget the other?

A blue dragon dove down, claws extended. And then another silver. Their talons grabbed Margo and the limp form of their father. Addie swooped across the waves and somehow picked up Sibby. Margo fought madly, but the blue dragon lifted her into the air and flew with vast wingbeats toward the crevice in the cliff. Holding their father, the silver followed. Addie came after, struggling a little, but holding the girl securely. Sibby seemed unconcerned and didn't squirm.

And then a bullet whined close to Jacob's wing.

Ryan! For a moment, Jacob soared higher. Below, like little crabs, the hunters scuttled this way and that on deck of the motorboat. The eyes of the crippled man who steered were wild with madness. A snarl rose to Jacob's lips. Ryan lifted his gun and another badly aimed bullet whizzed by. As the motorboat rocked on the waves, Jacob roared his fury and attacked. His claws raked the narrow canvas roof of the boat, shredding it. Beating his wings, Jacob rose twenty feet into the air.

With ferocious pleasure, he watched the screaming boys, remembering how they had laughed and hooted when Ryan tormented his victims. Every one of Ryan's gang jumped from the boat into the surf and began frantically stroking to shore, their life jackets bright orange splashes on the surging water.

"*Kill them!*" the cracked dragon voice screamed in his mind.

Yes! Jacob wanted them dead. Wanted Ryan's blood to spill in the water the way his father's blood had seeped into the grass. Wanted the muscle-bound idiot to feel the fear he had felt when the bully had tormented him. Wanted him to feel broken and useless.

The glorious power of revenge soared through Jacob. His enemy would feel small, would be crippled...would be forced into the half-life of fearful misery he had inflicted on others.

Jacob's mind roared with blood lust, with power. He could do anything. No one would ever harm him again. He relished the picture of the motorboat cracking against rocks, of Ryan falling to his knees.

"*Kill!*" screamed the voice.

Jacob dove at the boat, saw the crazy wheelchair man lift a gun, and with an easy swipe of his powerful claw, wrenched the weapon from his weak hands. The man was sobbing, tears blotching his face. Ryan clambered to his feet again, but terror etched his features.

Jacob hurled the gun into the water and prepared to dive again, to knock them both into the waves...to watch them bleed and drown.

He screamed rage and vengeance, circled high, and extended his claws. He saw his sister leave the dragon cave and fly toward him, her injured wing beating unevenly.

"*Jacob!*" Addie cried and circled below him.

Jacob growled frustration and tried to dodge past her, but she fluttered in his way.

"*Kill them! Kill the murderers!*" The mad voice of the white dragon screamed in their minds.

Below him, Jacob saw the hunter's terror. Saw that Ryan wept in helpless fear....

And suddenly, it was done.

Jacob refused to go that road, to become the biggest bully. Despite the pain they had caused him. Despite the humiliation they had dealt him. He would be bigger, grander.... He would not be small in his heart, no matter what his size or strength.

"*Maybe other people need you...*" His twin spoke in his mind.

Jacob shrugged his dragon shoulders and circled high, gathering his human and dragon thoughts together. Feeling like he had finally found himself again.

He circled slowly down to the boat, where

between cliff and waves, it rocked gently on the water. Reluctantly, he took his human form, felt the strength drain from his legs as he landed in the speedboat and faced Ryan.

"I'll get you!" Ryan bellowed, but his fists shook as he raised them.

Jacob held out his hand and allowed the sapphire glow of his dragon strength to surround him. "No," he said. "It's over. You c..can't fight us, Ryan. We're bigger, stronger, m..more intelligent. Go home while you can. It's over."

Without waiting for an answer, Jacob leapt up and winged through the air toward his dragon kin.

Looking back, he watched Ryan wrench the steering wheel from his raging uncle's grip, turn the craft around, and opening the throttle, race back toward the town.

Elation. Relief..."*We did it!*" Jacob soared upward, into the sky.

"*Jacob!*" Addie screamed. Confused, he backwinged and looked up.

Talons outstretched, the crystal dragon dove from the sky, shrieking her hatred. Bugling her blood lust.

Jacob dodged. Too late. The creature's claws missed his wings, but tore across his back.

Blinded by pain, Jacob beat his wings futilely. The beast dove at him again and again, slashing, clawing, ripping. Dimly he saw the other dragons hovering in a wide circle, silently watching. Waiting for his death.

Wingbeats above. He twisted. Dropped through the air to avoid the dragon queen. Recovered again.

How long could this go on? He was outmatched. If the white dragon shredded his wings, he would plunge into the water and drown.

Don't give up, he ordered himself. No matter what he'd faced, he'd never given up before and he wouldn't now.

Think, Jacob!

The pain. Hard to pull his thoughts together. He wouldn't surrender, not now, not when he had finally found freedom.

He fought the wind currents, trying to stay above the waves. Ahead the rocks rose like slavering teeth.

A plan...maybe... Jacob allowed himself to drop lower, to somehow glide just above the waves.

The crystal dragon trumpeted hatred and madness. Waves slapped Jacob's belly. Frantic, he reached for his sister's mind and pictured his desperate maneuver.

"*I got it, bro!*" His twin's voice answered.

"*The rocks...*" Jacob shot back.

"Keep low!"

Ignoring his pain, Jacob stayed just above the waves. Ahead, the rocks snaggle-toothed above the surf.

The crystal dragon howled in triumph. Jacob forced his exhausted wings to keep beating, ignored the weakness creeping across him as his blood dripped into the water. Determined. Not ever giving up...

The white dragon dove. As her talons clawed at him, Jacob seized the last of his strength and shot ahead. From high above, Addie dove down, clawing the beast's glittering hide, raking her from neck to tail.

Jacob circled back and as the white dragon tried to rise, he attacked alongside his sister. The mad beast twisted and snapped. Her fangs grazed Addie's leg, but Jacob smashed the slavering maw away. Addie tore at the dragon's wings until the tatters floated in the wind.

Still screaming with blood lust, the crystal dragon plunged into the surf. Her serpentine body twisted in the fierce waves and her blood streaked the foaming water until she smashed lifeless against the rocks.

And in his mind, in the minds of all the dragon kin, Jacob knew that the crystal dragon who had hunted them so mercilessly, was dead.

TWENTY-EIGHT

THE CIRCLE

ADDIE

Exhausted, Addie stared down at the spot in the water where the crystal dragon had disappeared. Raising her eyes, she looked at the silent ring of dragons, numbly wondering how she and Jacob could survive another attack.

They couldn't, she realized. Not with their injuries.

A large aquamarine blue dragon, swooped down towards them. His voice sounded in her mind, "*Come to the cave.*"

"*Well, he's not dive-bombing us,*" Addie thought at her twin.

She felt more than heard, Jacob's weary laugh. Then both of them tightened up in worry. She had left their dying father, injured mother, and the two girls in that cave. Addie wondered grimly if Margo had already started a brawl with the dragons inside.

Her wingbeats were awkward but she led Jacob toward the entrance to the cavern. The crenellated rock looked impassable, but she had seen how a cave hid behind the folds. Below them, raging waves smashed over jagged rocks. No boat could survive this passage, and the furrowed cliff face hid the the cavern from view from every angle.

Addie had been too desperate to save Sibby, her father, and her twin to pay attention to the cave, but now she looked around in wonder. Deep inside, the ocean was left behind and the cave opened up into a vast chamber. The farther in they flew, the greater the cavern. Glittering stalactites hung down from the ceiling and glowing stalagmites thrust up from the floor. The walls gleamed with crystal.

And then the floor opened up. Piled rocks gave the impression of nests. Dragons of all sizes watched their approach. Addie ignored them, scanning the area for her family and friends.

There. To one side of the cave, Margo crouched with her arms around her sister. Her narrowed eyes constantly scanned any dragons who ventured near them. She had pulled a few sharp rocks into a pile beside her.

Not far from her, Addie's mother, in human form again, held their father's head in her lap, her face covered with tears, her arms held awkwardly.

"*Mom!*" the cry broke from Jacob. He dropped to the floor beside her, rapidly changing back into human shape. He grabbed their mother, and hugged her.

Addie circled and then landed, letting herself slowly morph back into human form. She didn't know whether to run to her mother, or yell at her. Maybe both.

"Addie?" her mom called. "Oh sweetheart, is it you?"

Then Addie saw that her mother couldn't lift her arms. All her anger drained away, and with a cry of pity, she ran to her.

"I'm so sorry," her mother wept. "I'm so sorry. The dragon queen, Clia, broke my wings when I tried to come back to you."

Addie hugged her, sobbing, ignoring the tears streaming down her own face. And then the anger took her again. She stood up, and raging, faced the watching dragons.

"I'd like to kill you," she yelled. "What are you? My mother is one of you! My father said dragons help people! You're nothing but savage animals!"

The dragons shifted uncomfortably. Addie sensed anger, resentment...fear.

And then the blue dragon stalked forward, head lowered. "I am Nor. With the death of

Clia I am now clan leader. And you are right, my daughter," he said sadly.

"I'm not your daughter!" Addie shouted. She ignored the pain and balled her hands into fists. She didn't care how ridiculous she was being. "What happened to the legacy of Knukor? You should be noble! Not hiding in caves like sewer rats."

She felt the dragon anger building around her and she didn't care. With his dragging step, Jacob moved beside her.

Nor's lips drew back in a snarl, but then Addie felt him reach into the minds of all the dragons, herself and Jacob included. Distantly, she felt the touch of others....

"You did not know the terror of the pogrom," Nor said, his voice a low growl. "Our mates, our children, our hatchlings slaughtered as we tried to serve. But Clia, daughter of Knukor, rose in anger and led us into this bitter exile. For many, many years she has been a great leader and so our clan escaped the murders. She bargained for safe passage with the Vikings and we have stayed here, safe, all these centuries...until Audra disobeyed and brought the hunters back upon us."

Dragon and human heads turned towards Addie's mother. She sat silently, eyes downcast, shoulders drooping.

"Because of her," the dragon said wearily, "we are no longer safe. The war has begun again."

"*No!* No more!" Fists clenched, Margo sprang to her feet. "I'm the last of the dragon-slayers," she shouted. "And I saved two of your kind. The war is *over.*" She paused, and Addie saw tears were running down her face. "It's over. There is no one left to hunt you. Except me." She spread her arms, showing her empty hands. "Except me."

Addie watched with awe as Margo stood straight, chin up. Nor thrust his glittering, fanged head toward her. Only a tremor in the warrior's body showed her fear.

"The war is over," Addie echoed fiercely. Limping, she went to stand beside Margo, shoulders touching.

"It's d..done," Jacob shouted. He dragged himself over to stand beside them.

"It's time to weave the threads." Sibby's singsong voice floated through the cavern. "But the man is dying...."

"*Dad!*" Addie called and forgetting the dragons, ran to her father. He lay motionless, white. She turned back to the dragons. "You have to see it's over. Help us the way dragons have always helped...please!"

For a moment the cavern was utterly silent.

The time of Clio is over, whispered across the dragon minds. *There is a better way.* Words drifted in their minds from far away, from long ago.

"It's over," Addie echoed, pleading. "Help us."

She felt a sigh move through the dragon minds. Decision. Acceptance. With slow steps, as though something wonderful was being remembered, the dragons formed a narrow circle around the humans. The twins' mother and father lay in the center. Addie and Jacob crouched beside them. Margo swept up her unresisting sister, and white-faced, moved until she too stood beside the Medways. Sibby waited silently, a small smile on her face, as she regarded the encircling dragons.

Addie and Jacob felt the dragons' memories stir and come alive. The whisper became a song. Other voices, soft and distant joined the melody. The twins felt the power growing, uniting, until it echoed the harmony of the universe. Then the dragons began to blow gently on them, their breath smelling sweetly of burnt sugar. Dreamily, Addie watched her mother's hair lift and flutter. Then she closed her eyes and soared with the song. As she flew within forever, she heard her father groan softly as her mother whispered his name.

As the tendrils of song and the aroma of burnt sugar twined around her, Addie felt the pain from her injuries drain away. Beside her, Jacob gasped. Vaguely, she was aware that his wounds were mending and strength flowed into him. A long sigh escaped from Sibby; a sob broke from Margo, who held her.

And then the song was done and the magic eased away.

Sweetly exhausted, Addie slipped down onto the stone floor. She was mildly aware of some kind of covering, of a warm body heating the stone beneath her and the air around her. Of a sense of utter peace and safety.

Hours later, she shook her head and groggily looked around. Her brother, parents and Sibby slept. Each covered, each lying close to the side of a drowsing dragon. The green dragon she and Jacob had saved, healed now, blinked at her sleepily.

Only Margo appeared wide awake. The once dragon-slayer sat cross-legged in front of Nor, the two of them deep in conversation.

A moment later, Addie saw her twin sit up. She moved over to crouch beside him, looking anxiously. His wounds were clearly healed, but the larger question....

"I...I'm better," Jacob said. Awkwardly he moved his weak legs. Addie held his arm while he stood. "Not completely better."

"Maybe Nor...?" Addie whispered.

Jacob nodded, and with Addie's help, the twins went over to where Margo talked with Nor and sat beside her.

"My brother still isn't fixed," Addie said. "Can you heal him? I mean his wounds are gone, but his crippled legs?"

The blue dragon shook his head wearily. "We have healed all your wounds, and to the broken ones, we have given some strength and a little healing, but we can't change the way they are made." His eyes sought out Sibby, still peacefully sleeping. Addie felt Margo tense beside her. "Your human body is not formed for strength, Jacob. We can't remake you. The little one is the same. We have smoothed the tangles in her mind, but we cannot change her."

Addie wanted to shout at Nor to gather the dragons, to order them to try again. But her dragon heart knew he was speaking the truth.

Beside her, Jacob stared down at the ground, then lifted his head. "I have strength and power as a dragon," Jacob said. "But as a human, I'm crippled...will always be crippled."

"Yes," Nor agreed. "If you stay among us, you will always be strong and fierce, able to ride the winds and dive into ancient knowledge."

To her surprise, Addie saw Jacob begin to laugh. “But you don’t have hamburgers or milkshakes....”

The look of confusion on the dragon’s face was almost humanly comical. Addie felt herself laugh in response, and she wasn’t even sure why.

Jacob let out a deep sigh. “Seems that no matter what choice I make, I lose something huge.”

“At least you get a choice,” Margo said tartly. “All I’ve got is my crazy uncle and disgusting brother waiting for me.” Her eyes strayed to her sister, waking now. “My mother’s nice, and there’s Sibby.”

Addie felt the other voices reaching for her. Old voices, calm, gentle voices...calling.

“Are there other dragons?” she asked suddenly. “Other colonies that escaped the hunts?”

Nor’s brows pulled together. “We have heard voices...” he hissed. “Renegades who live among humans in the far north. Clio commanded us to close our minds to their voices.”

“And Clio’s made such great decisions,” Addie snapped. Without waiting for Nor’s response, she opened her thoughts. Eagerly she reached out to the distant dragon minds that had spoken to her...and the knowledge of them rushed in. She took a long, shuddering breath.

"Alaska," she whispered. "They are in Alaska...and they want us! They have been trying to find us!"

She saw Jacob's head snap up, saw the sapphire sheen on his skin as he opened his dragon mind to the voices.

"Silver Claw!" he cried. "They have a town where people and dragons live together...and you're right, Addie." She saw tears in his eyes. "They want us! I won't be a freak. I can be human and dragon...I can be both."

They felt Margo shifting away from them. Addie reached out and laid a hand on her friend's arm. "You too," she said. "You can come. You and Sibby...and your mother. Find out the truth."

Margo's face twisted into a sneer. "Like they'd want a St. George."

Nor's face moved to within a few inches of Margo's face. "They call us." The burnt sugar scent of his breath drifted over them all. "They offer a home to all of us. We are refugees from a long war...and they offer a home and peace."

Addie put her arm around Margo's shoulders as the girl began to sob. Jacob leaned against her. "I..it'll be good," he murmured.

Margo straightened suddenly and wiped her forearm against her blotched face. "Yeah, why not," she said. "Mom always said she wanted to go back to Anchorage."

Addie drew a long, quivering breath. "It's going to be great," she said as her eyes strayed over to her parents, sitting quietly together now, happiness glowing in their faces. She shoulder bumped Jacob. "And, hey bro – we finally have somewhere for our totally weird family to belong...and I think it's time to go there!"

Jacob grinned and hoisted himself to his feet. "And the d..dragons?" he asked.

Nor lifted his glittering blue head. "All of us will go," he agreed. "Dragon kin and their champions. It is time to go home."

AND NOW A SNEAK PEEK AT

DRAGONS OF FROST AND FIRE

"I know she's still alive!"

A year ago her mother disappeared in an Alaskan blizzard, but Kit Soriano refuses to give up. Against all logic, propelled by recurring dreams of ice-white dragons and a magical silver knife, Kit journeys to the wilderness town of Silver Claw where her mother vanished. She's clearly not welcome, but her knife throbs with heat and her dreams show the impossible – mythical dragons are guarding her sleeping mother.

Desperate, Kit has no choice but to rely on Dai, who knows more than he says about the wild magic rippling beneath the surface of the town. She wants to trust him. But is he her friend or an enemy? If she's wrong, will she too be lost forever in the unforgiving Alaskan wilderness?

DRAGONS OF DESERT AND DUST

A boy with the heart of a Dragon...

Fourteen-year-old Angel Cerillos is stuck living with foster parents at a second-rate desert motel while his mother is in the hospital. Despite threats from a local rancher and his greedy foster father, Angel is determined to scour the harsh desert for turquoise nuggets that could pay for his mom's care. Without them, all he has of value is a carved, two-headed turquoise serpent, left to him by his mysterious father. It's a hard life. But the desert spirits are awakening, and the mythic power of his dragon talisman spins Angel into terrifying danger.

DRAGONS OF FROST AND FIRE

DRAGONS OF EARTH, WATER, FIRE AND AIR

ONE

The floatplane touched down on Silver Lake, spewing sheets of water into the air. Pressing her icy hands against the passenger window, Kit Soriano tried to force back a shudder. This far north, the Rocky Mountains peaks thrust into the sky like teeth – old teeth, cruel teeth, with glacial lips pulled back into a snarl.

"Silver Claw," the pilot called over his shoulder. "Last stop of humanity."

David Soriano peered out his own window, then reached his hand across the seat to grip his daughter's cold fingers. Silently they stared at this terrible place where they had come to find answers. Beyond the narrow beach, a few weather-beaten buildings made up the town. Past that, mountainous ice caps blended into clouds in every direction. At the north end of the lake, a glacier hundreds of feet high lay between the mountains like a mythic sleeping monster. Aqua and blue ice shone translucent in the sunlight.

"This is what mom tried to describe...." Kit gripped the dragon-shaped knife hidden in her pocket – she was going to need every ounce of magic her mother had said it possessed. There was nothing else left for her to believe in.

The pilot eased the plane to the dock and cut the engine. Kit's ears still thrummed with the vibrations, when a series of rumbles and cracks rolled across the lake and through the skin of the plane. An ice monolith slowly split from the glacier and crashed into the water. Spray shot a hundred feet into the air. Shock waves raced across the lake, rocking the plane.

When Kit gasped and clutched the armrests, the pilot laughed. "That's Silver Snake Glacier." He pointed to the ice cliff. "In spring it breaks up some – calving, it's called. But you've never heard anything like the roars and howls that come from that ice snake in winter. I was holed up here one year when an early blizzard rolled in. I swear I thought the noise alone would kill me."

Kit forced herself to stare impassively at the forbidding Alaskan landscape. "I'm not afraid of noise." She would not, would not let this place defeat her.

The pilot shrugged. "Hope you're not planning to stay too long," he warned. "Once winter gets her talons into this country, it can cost you your life to go outside of town."

"We'll be back in New York by winter," her father said. "We're only staying a couple of weeks."

Until we find her, Kit vowed.

The pilot heaved himself out of his chair, wrestled with the door, and showed them how to scramble down to the pontoon and then jump onto the dock. Kit shivered. Even though it was mid-August, the Alaskan air was cold through her fleece vest. She warmed up a little as they unloaded their gear.

A dozen of the town's residents drifted down to the dock, but Kit kept her eyes off the kids. Those kids had lured her mother to Silver Claw – nearly a quarter of them were albino, a genetic mutation. Dr. Nora Reits had been a genetics researcher. Nearly a year ago, she had disappeared without a trace in an early fall storm in Silver Claw.

Kit again touched the silver pocketknife nestled in her pocket. Magic find her, she prayed silently. Warmth tingled against her skin – the connection was still strong. Relieved, Kit turned her energy to separating their gear from the supplies ordered by the residents.

A lot of folks were on the dock now. In spite of herself, Kit sneaked a look under her lashes. The albino kids had snow-white hair and glacier blue eyes. Unlike some albino people, their sparkling glances showed good eyesight and they glowed with health.

"Dr. Soriano?" A big man with red hair stuck out his hand to Kit's father. "I'm Pat Kelly, mayor of this place. I wish I could welcome you here under better circumstances."

Dr. Soriano shook hands with the mayor. "We appreciate your willingness to let us get some closure on my wife's disappearance."

The mayor nodded. "I understand your feelings. We lost one of our own boys in that blizzard. This is a hard land – beautiful, but hard."

"Yes," Dr. Soriano said gazing at the ring of jagged peaks. "But I'm hoping the clinic will be a useful return for your hospitality."

"My mother-in-law will keep you busy, even if no one else does," Pat replied with an easy smile. "It's a long flight to Anchorage when the problems are the aches and pains old folks feel every time the weather changes."

As Kit reached up to grab the rest of their bags, she drew a deep breath. After all the setbacks and problems, she could hardly believe they were really here.

It had taken her father weeks to work out their journey. Getting to Silver Claw would be no problem – a regular flight from New York City to Anchorage and then they could book seats on the floatplane that delivered supplies to the town every couple of weeks. But inquiries about where to stay had been discouraging. There was apparently no reliable Internet connection that far north, and so all communication was by snail mail. A letter from the town council, signed Mary McGough, Secretary, had been brusque. The council regretted there was no hotel in Silver Claw.

Dr. Soriano's lips had thinned as he read the letter aloud to Kit.

"Isn't she the person Mom rented a room and office from? Wasn't it above a store or something?" Kit had asked.

"Yup," her dad said. "Let's try this one more time." That evening, he wrote back politely requesting that he and his daughter rent the room that his wife had previously occupied.

Three weeks later a second response from the town secretary stated that she was using the space Dr. Reits had rented for storage and so it was no longer available.

"I don't think they want us," Dr. Soriano had told his daughter over macaroni and cheese.

"I don't care. You promised me..." Kit looked challengingly into his eyes.

“And I keep my promises,” he’d said. “Have some salad. It’s only a little brown.”

After dinner, while Kit had loaded the dishwasher and then tackled physics homework, he had written a third letter to the town council.

Dear Members of the Council,

I am hoping that we will still be able to work out the details of my daughter’s and my visit. We are coming to Silver Claw. As east coast city people, we don’t have a lot of experience with wilderness camping, but we will come with tents and backpacks and set up on the glacier itself, if necessary.

However, I have a proposal for you. I am a medical doctor and I’m willing to operate a free clinic for the residents of the area in return for accommodation and supplies while my daughter and I are in town.

We will be arriving on August 12th, with or without a place to stay.

Sincerely,

David Soriano, M.D.

The next response came from Pat Kelly instead of the secretary and it was a lot friendlier. A new cabin had been built for his family and he was willing to let Kit and her dad use it for a couple of weeks. He sympathized with the Soriano's need to see the town where Dr. Reits had spent her last few weeks. The residents of the town would be pleased to welcome them.

Kit and her dad flew from New York on August 11th, spent the night in Anchorage and the next morning boarded the small floatplane.

After all her thinking and worrying, it seemed to Kit that she was in a dream as she stood at the edge of the dock and gazed across the wild landscape. The glacier glinted, shifting colors like a living, crystal animal.

Mayor Kelly turned from Dr. Soriano to the people standing on the dock behind him. "Here, you kids give a hand. Kirsi...Dai...grab some of the bags."

Two of the older albino teenagers, a girl and boy, left the group. Both were tall and strong, their white-blonde hair ruffling in the steady breeze. They radiated health and were incredibly good looking. Mesmerized, Kit realized with a small shock that they were better than good looking – they were the most beautiful teens she had ever seen. They were graceful, perfectly proportioned, and there wasn't even a zit to be seen. Kit thought she could hate them just for that.

As Kirsi leaned down to pick up luggage, she turned cold blue eyes toward Kit. "You shouldn't have come here," she hissed. "You soft city people don't belong." She hoisted the heavy pack over her shoulder with ease and strode away without a backward glance.

The breeze off the lake quickened. Kit shivered.

"You'll get used to the temperatures," Dai said beside her. He appeared about seventeen, a year older than she was. Up close, Kit thought his looks alone could warm her up.

Kit made a grab for her peace of mind and shrugged. "I'm not afraid of the cold."

"That's good because sometimes we get a lot of it. I'm Dai Phillips." He stuck out his hand to shake.

Kit hesitated a split second, then shook his hand. It was so very warm and firm. A responding flash of heat shot through her. This was not normal for her at all.

"I'm Kit." At home the kids either didn't touch or did hand slaps and fist bumps. Nobody under forty shook hands.

Patrick Kelly picked up one of Dr. Soriano's medical cases. "We do appreciate your willingness to run a health clinic even for two weeks, Doc," he said. "Hey there, Jancy. You, Mikey. Help the doctor with his bags." Two red-haired children each picked up a suitcase. "Dai, are you going to stand around all day or are you going to help that little girl out?"

Hot color flushed Dai's face. "Yes, Uncle Pat," he said under his breath. He reached for a duffel. "This yours, Kit?"

"I'll get it," she said. "I packed it. I can carry it." She hoisted it up and over her thin shoulder. "And I'm sixteen...not a little girl." She knew she looked too young and fragile to be in the wilderness. But she also knew that her slender bones were connected to tough muscle.

"Okay," Dai said. "But it's a bit of a hike to the cabin and I'm used to the path."

"Whatever." Kit slid the bag back to the dock, refusing to allow even a flicker of relief to cross her face. She'd jammed it with everything she thought might be useful – survival gear, guidebooks, contour maps, compass, and a Swiss Army knife.

Dai's deep blue eyes searched her own.

"What?" Kit demanded. His intense gaze unnerved her.

Dai leaned over and lifted the bag like it weighed six ounces instead of sixty pounds. "It's good you've come to us – you're the kind that's called."

"Called? Called what?"

"Called by the mountains and wilderness. By the heart that beats up there." Again, his eyes pierced her own. "Your mother was the same. You both belong here. I feel it."

Kit felt a lump rise sharply in her throat so she turned away and stared at the town as though fascinated by the worn clapboard structures. Kirsi stood at the top of the path, arms folded, looking stonily down at the people on the dock. Kit stared back defiantly.

"My mother didn't belong here and I don't either," she turned and told Dai. "I'm going to find out what happened to her and then you'll never see me again."

She picked up a bag and marched up the path toward Kirsi. Other men and children took the rest of the luggage. The remainder of the people finished unloading boxes of supplies from the plane and began hauling them up the hill toward town. Dai strode after her, whistling off-key. Kit glanced back at him. She had never seen anyone so vibrantly alive. And he had talked about her mother. Had he gotten to know her? Would he have information that would lead Kit to her?

Abruptly she slowed down, matching her steps to his. But with a cool glance, he trudged faster away from her, still whistling. Kit's eyes narrowed, but she followed without comment. In a moment she had reached Kirsi. The girl looked her over like she was a dead fish washed onto the shore.

"Stay away from Dai. He has no use for your kind," Kirsi mocked.

"What kind is that, Kirsi?" Kit demanded.

The girl's lips curled into a sneer. "A weak outlander. You'll be very sorry you ever came here." She shoved past Kit, knocking her off balance.

Regaining her footing, Kit glared after her. "I think you will be surprised." She made no effort to catch up, waiting instead for her dad and the others.

"The house is this way, Doctor." Mayor Kelly gestured along an overgrown dirt road that edged the lake. "The clinic building is in town, but this cabin has an incredible view of Silver Snake."

The cabin sat on a rounded hill overlooking the lake. The building was made of shaped logs, with a fresh look about them. Shuttered windows along the sides were wide and evenly spaced. A long porch was angled to face the glacier.

Everyone trooped through the screen door, but Kit dropped her bag and leaned on the railing, looking towards mountains and ice. Behind her, voices filled the cabin. But out here, the stillness folded into a sense of being on the edge of another world. Kit breathed deeply, tasting the tang of wilderness, and another acrid scent – sweet and bitter mingled. She tossed her head to let the clean air wash over her. After the long despair, she was coming alive again. Kit remembered how her mother had described this place in her letters....

Silver Snake Glacier drapes the mountains like a huge sleeping animal. It really seems alive, shifting with every color that ever existed. I hope you get to see it some day – it must be one of the wonders of the world! I am going to hike up there and see if I can fathom its secrets. Something that otherworldly must have secrets, Kit. Devin tells me the glacier is riddled with crevasses and caves – a beautiful but deadly creature, I guess. It wakes when the winter storms howl over the mountains....

Dai came out on the porch and stood beside her. Despite herself, Kit was too aware of the warmth he radiated. Of those broad shoulders and lithe build. She'd never been this aware of the boys at home. Pheromones. He must be radiating mutated pheromones and she was feeling every one of them.

Another crack shattered the quiet of the town.

"Loud, isn't it?" Kit said turning to him. She froze. His eyes were a deeper blue. She'd swear they had darkened. Ridiculous. Even weird eyes, genetically mutated eyes, shouldn't change color. It had to be a trick of the light.

"This is a great time of year to be in Silver Claw." Dai's expression once again lightened to an easy smile. "There's hiking, hunting and fishing during the day and bonfires and get-togethers at night. Mary McGough at the general store gets in movies now and then."

"Sounds terrific," Kit said, "But I already have plans." She forced herself to turn away from those hot, mesmerizing eyes and look back at the cold waters of the lake. Her mother had said native legends put some kind of mythic beast in those cold depths.

Then Dai's hand, hot and strong, gripped her arm. "There are no other plans in Silver Claw," Dai told her. "You'll be smart to listen to me." The warning in his voice was unmistakable.

"Or what?" Kit challenged. How friendly or how dangerous was this guy? He was like fire and ice. Already this place was freaking her out, all beauty and danger.

His eyes shifted even darker, making that weird sense of warmth flare through her again. She didn't know whether he would have answered or not because they were interrupted by the door swinging open. The moment bled away.

"Kit," her dad called. "Which bedroom do you want?"

"Excuse me," Kit stepped past Dai and followed her father.

Inside, several men and women had settled on the sofas and chairs. Dai came in after her and crossed over to Kirsi who leaned against the far wall. As they stood talking in quiet voices and sometimes glancing in her direction, Kit felt another surge of anger. Were they talking about her? And why should she care?

In the meantime, two women were opening and shutting the cupboard doors in the kitchen area, calling on Dr. Soriano to admire how thoroughly they had stocked up for him.

"My wife is bringing some lasagna over," the mayor said. "A bit of a welcome to let you get yourself unpacked and settled tonight."

"Dr. Soriano," Dai struck in, "my mother said I'm to ask you for dinner tomorrow at seven, if you don't have other plans.... " He glanced mockingly at Kit.

"Great," Dr. Soriano said. "That's very kind. We'll be there. Now Kit, what about that bedroom?"

Three bedrooms opened off the kitchen-dining-living area, so Kit chose one where the window faced the glacier. While her dad chatted with the people who had helped bring their belongings up, Kit hauled in her bags. Methodically, she unpacked her clothing and filled the drawers of the wooden dresser. She left all her survival gear in the duffel bag, zipped it up, and pushed it far under the bed.

"Kit!" her dad called. "The most marvelous dinner is being spread out here for us!"

The main room was packed with big, loud strangers. It seemed like everyone who had come down to the dock had migrated up to the cabin and brought a few friends along. Did any of those open, friendly faces hide the secret of her mother's disappearance? She wanted to shout at them, demand they tell her what they knew, but instead she forced herself to paste on a fake smile.

"Please, you must stay," her father was urging.

With only a brief show of reluctance, everyone dug into the lasagna, salad, bread and meat that all seemed to have magically appeared. Kit picked among the dishes and settled in the remotest corner of the sofa. Dai left Kirsi and perched on the arm beside her.

Ignoring him, Kit took a bite of the dark meat. Flavor exploded in her senses.

"Backstrap," Dai said. "The tenderest and tastiest part of a moose."

Kit put her fork down but chewed on. It was good – different from anything else she'd tasted. "Great!" she mumbled through her full mouth.

"You're honored," Dai said. "That's probably the last of Uncle Pat's winter store. He's the best hunter in town, but we try to only hunt moose in the fall and winter."

Kit cut another piece of meat and popped it in her mouth. "The only moose I ever saw for real was in a zoo. It was big and sad looking so it seems cruel to hunt them."

"We have to eat and there aren't many fast food restaurants in the wilderness," Dai replied. "Besides, those hamburgers don't come from carrots."

Kit took a big bite of her bread to avoid answering. She knew he was right, but she didn't want to acknowledge that the rules were different here in Silver Claw. With mountains, lakes and glaciers surrounding them, they hunted to eat. They killed to survive.

A burst of laughter filled the cabin. She tried another bite of backstrap. It tasted fine on her tongue. Kit looked around at all the handsome, strong faces. She would learn what they knew, she vowed. And if they had secrets, she would find them.

Despite their protests about letting the Sorianos unpack, the townspeople didn't leave for hours. By the time Kit could finally get to bed, she was too wound up to sleep.

Outside, twilight had eased over the land, casting the mountains into dark relief. The luminous hands on her watch read 11:03 but the sky still shone dusky blue. Kit sat on her bed, wrapped in a quilt, looking out toward Silver Snake Glacier.

It drew her, called her, just as Dai had said it would. Her mom's letters had described the hours she spent hiking by the glacier. She'd written that the sight and sound of the ancient ice relieved her frustrations when the townspeople refused to cooperate with her research.

And that's how I'll start, Kit decided; she would go to the places her mother had described, try to find some kind of clue her mother may have left behind. Looking out the open window at the immense distances and peaks, Kit wondered with a sinking heart whether she would be able to find the places from the descriptions in the letters. In New York, hemmed in by buildings and streetlights, she had not been able to grasp the vastness of the landscape.

Her father came in, set a lantern on the table beside her bed and sat down.

"They seem like nice people around here," he said at last.

Kit rolled her eyes. "That's what Mom said...until they found out what she was doing."

Her hand slipped under her pillow to touch the knife and the packet of letters. In the last one, Nora Reits had written in an excited scrawl from her office over the general store. She had said she would try to slip the letter into the outgoing mail sack before the floatplane arrived. This flight, she was sure, would bring lab results for the blood samples she had coaxed from one albino boy. Kit got the letter two days after her mother disappeared.

"Kit, it was a simple hiking accident," her dad said. "You know she hiked up there alone, even though the weather was threatening."

"Then why did the lab results disappear?" Kit demanded. "And the searchers didn't find a body. They're keeping her somewhere. I know it! My knife...."

"Kit, don't start about that knife again." Her father rubbed his hand over his face; his eyes were exhausted. Kit fell silent.

If only he would believe what Kit knew against all reason was true. Her mother was alive.

Another crack reverberated through the air. The lantern flickered. Somewhere, out there, Kit knew her mother was alive.

DRAGONS OF DESERT AND DUST

DRAGONS OF EARTH, WATER, FIRE AND AIR

ONE

Facing east toward the mountains, Angel Cerillos dug his toes into the loose slats of the shed's roof. As the sun shimmered across the New Mexico desert, he lifted his arms upward, feeling the turquoise talisman warming against his chest like a piece of desert sky.

"The eagles are my brothers..." he chanted. He swept his arms downward in the eagles' curving wing thrusts, imitating how they soared over the parched mountains.

"I am greater than the eagles..."

Eyes drifting shut, his mind flew skyward.

"I am king of the skies.... " The rhythmic beat, beat of his arms echoed the chant. He could hear the singing clearly now – there, just beyond the horizon. A thrumming chant that was getting louder and louder, day by day. Magic singing that no one else heard....

"Angel! *Angel!*" Treese Tanner's voice cracked through the dream. Arms still flapping, his feet skidded on the tin roof. Scrabbling with fingers and scraping with toes, he slid along the burning metal, and then down over the edge.

A cry tore from his throat. He flew now, but straight down, slamming onto the hard-packed dirt. Gasping for breath, he saw his foster mother loom like a black shadow against the sky. Treese Tanner's lips pursed and she jammed her big hands on her hips. The hot wind blew her badly-cut hair around her head like a faded halo.

"Y'okay?" she asked.

Angel tried to answer, but all that came out was a raspy grunt.

"Can you get up?" she demanded.

He wheezed again, and thrashed like a bug on a pin. She stared back, exasperation evident on her weathered face. "You deserve to have broke every bone you got," she told him. "Fourteen years old and you don't have the sense you were born with. And those sad blue eyes of yours don't fool me. I seen the way you look at Gary when he pushes you too far. But you watch yourself around him – he can get mean."

"I know," Angel grunted. "I ain't gonna get in his way."

Treese snorted. "I don't think you'd hardly know anything, the way you're always mooning around."

"I can look after myself." Angel stared up at the sky, wishing he could fly up there and away from his life.

"You need someone to watch out for you, kid, but I'm not the mothering kind, so you be careful. Now, get up. Put your shirt on. We got work to do." She turned and headed toward the front of the motel. Angel stayed where he was, lying in the dust, waiting for his breathing to get back to normal.

For a moment he had thought his secret chant was going to work, thought that the haunting dreams and whispering voices would be satisfied and stop. His only friend around here, Celsa Reyna, had helped him come up with words that sounded like an old Indian chant. He had even come out here early – not sunrise exactly – but as close as he could manage without an alarm clock. Spitting out a mouthful of dust, Angel sat up and stared into the gleaming blue sky. For a minute he had felt like he could flap his arms and rise into the air just like one of the eagles that soared over the motel. Felt like he could escape.

"*Angel!*" Treese called from the front of the motel. "Get a move on!"

"Coming!" Angel yelled back, even though he stayed put, looking up at the sky, drinking in the beautiful blue. For once he felt peaceful, not all torn up by the storms of emotion that rolled over him like thunderclouds on the mountains. Up until the state moved him here to the Lone Butte Motel he had been able to pull back, not get caught up in the fights and bad stuff around him. But there was something about this clean dry air, endless horizon, and blue sky that had him stirred up. Of course, life at the motel didn't help.

Treese sounded gruff, but she was all right. Angel mostly liked her. But his foster father, Gary, was a whole different deal. He could make anyone laugh with his jokes. His voice was silky and smooth. Everyone liked Gary. Everyone but Angel...and maybe Treese too, though she never said.

With a sigh, Angel got to his feet. He shook back his straight brown hair, tried to dust off his skin, then gave up and pulled on the loose shirt that was one of Gary's hand-me-downs. His foster father would be back from town soon with another case of beer. If the motel's rooms weren't clean and the beds changed, he'd be mad. That would mean the silky voice would get hard and if he'd already started on the beer, maybe he'd stop joking and start slapping.

For a moment Angel gripped the turquoise talisman – the only thing that he had left from his own family. His fingers traced the two-headed, horned snake, more like a dragon, with its long sinewy body looped back and forth and a fanged head on each end. Angel had had it as long as he could remember, strung on string or an old shoelace around his neck. "You keep that safe," his ma had told him. "It's your birth gift from your father."

And he did keep it safe. It never left him, no matter what. He'd figured there was some invisible magic on it because no one ever said anything about it and no matter how chaotic his foster homes were, the other kids never grabbed for it. They just looked and then their eyes slid away like they forgot they saw it. And mostly Angel forgot too. But a few months ago, around his fourteenth birthday, there had been a change. Sometimes, the carving seemed to hum like the high voltage wires that swayed high above the highway. When Angel held the dragon in his two hands, he'd felt a jolt of power. Everything he saw, heard, smelled and tasted seemed brighter, cleaner...more beautiful. His head swam and he felt himself soaring into ideas and visions that were new and frightening. And then... nothing. They just faded away. He didn't know whether to be terrified or thrilled. But those feelings had compelled him to try the Indian chant thing. Dumb.

"*Angel!*" The sharpened note in Treese's voice meant she'd spotted Gary's truck on the horizon.

"*Coming!*" Angel shoved the talisman under his shirt and sprinted towards the motel. He rounded the building's cracked adobe wall and grabbed the laundry cart he'd left by number18. By the time Gary's truck spun gravel into a cloud out on the parking lot, Angel was head first into the room's shower stall, scrubbing. The bed was stripped and the soiled laundry in the cart. Crisp, clean sheets that Treese had ironed last night were on the bed, and the faded bedspread had been smoothed over them.

Angel felt rather than saw Gary's presence in the doorway. He scrubbed harder, not looking up, knowing that even a glance might invite some kind of punishment if Gary was in a punishing mood.

"Well, can't you say hi?" Gary demanded.

Angel sat back on his heels and wiped his arm across his brow, hoping it would impress his foster father with how hard he was working. The man was big, a football player in his high school glory days, but now most of the muscle had slid down to his gut.

"Hi, Gary. I was scrubbing so I didn't hear you come in." Angel eyed the bottle of beer in the man's hand and kept his face carefully blank.

His foster father grunted. Before he turned to go, he shoved his big knee into Angel's shoulder blades, sending the boy sprawling head first into the shower stall. The cleaner streaked across Angel's cheek, burning. Scrambling back out onto the cracked tile, he used his shirt sleeve to wipe the soap from his face.

"Watch you don't slip there, boy." Gary snickered and sauntered out. "And move your butt," he called back. "If you want any lunch, all these rooms better be clean."

Angel slowly wiped his face again. His skin stung, and the earlier spurt of anger fanned into fury. He wished, he wished with everything he had, that Gary would be on the receiving end – just once. His hand crept to the turquoise dragon. The talisman burned in his hand, hotter and hotter. Angel shut his eyes and wished and wished.

A white convertible streaks toward the motel...a writhing shape skitters up from the dust devils that whirl across the road...the car swerves...spins into the Lone Butte parking lot... gravel shoots everywhere like dusty bullets... and Gary walks out of number 18, beer bottle tilted up. He doesn't see the spinning car....

The driver wrenches the wheel. The fender just side-swipes Gary, sending him sprawling in the dirt. The bottle flies from his hand, shattering on the stones, shooting shards of glass in all directions....

Treese's cry shocked Angel from the dream. He dropped the talisman back under his shirt and tore outside to see what was going on. Gary was sprawled in the dust, his hand clapped to his cheek. A trickle of blood oozed between his fingers. Broken glass glinted in the gravel and beer steamed away in the desert heat.

A big man in a suit and cowboy hat rushed from the sports car toward Gary. Treese came pelting from number seven. Angel pressed back against the motel wall, breathing hard.

"You all right?" the man asked, squatting by Gary.

"You crazy fool," Gary sputtered. "You coulda killed me." He wiped his arm across his cheek, leaving a streak of blood on his sleeve.

"I really am sorry," the man said. "I thought I saw an animal on the road, so I cranked the wheel and my car spun right out of control. That's never happened with this car before. I don't understand it. But are you all right? Should I take you into the hospital in Santa Fe?"

Gary struggled to his feet. The stranger rose beside him, offering a steadying hand.

Gary shrugged it away. "No, I don't need no doctors. I'm okay." He eyed the man and his pale eyes sharpened. "Say, aren't you John Hydemann? You own the Turquoise Hill Ranch, right?"

Angel sucked in his breath. The Turquoise Hill Ranch bounded the back of the motel. And kept on going to cover hundreds of square miles more – one of the biggest ranches in the state. Celsa and several other kids at school lived in the adobe cottages Hydemann had built for his hired hands. She called him King Hydemann because everyone jumped to do what he said.

"That's right. I'm John Hydemann." The rancher held out his hand.

Gary grinned, wiped his palm on his jeans, and stuck out his own hand. "And I'm Gary Tanner. Don't know why we haven't met before, being neighbors. I own and operate this here Lone Butte Motel." He motioned grandly. "It ain't much at the moment, but we're fixing it up. I plan to turn it into a resort and conference center – I'm thinkin' of an Anasazi kinda pueblo theme. But I'm looking for the right business partners. Men with vision. Like me and you...."

"Can I offer you some iced tea, Mr. Hydemann?" Treese interrupted. Angel could see the embarrassed flush on his foster mother's face.

Gary stiffened, but he kept the smile going.

"No, I thank you though." Mr. Hydemann nodded to her. "I have an appointment that I'm already late for. And if you're sure you're not hurt, Mr. Tanner...." He offered his hand in a farewell shake.

"Gary, call me Gary!" He shook hands. "I think I'm just fine. Been a pleasure to meet you, John." He leaned on the back fender of the gleaming white car like a good-natured pal.

As Hydemann turned to get into the car, he spotted Angel standing in the shadows. To Angel's amazement, the rancher smiled and included him in his wave. Angel didn't move, but felt a brief surge of pleasure at being noticed.

That pleasure dulled his wits. He stayed when he should have slipped away, because as soon as the car became a white blur on the straight road, the friendly mask dropped from Gary's heavy face.

"Iced tea?" he demanded. "Treese, you stupid cow! A man like John Hydemann don't waste his time on iced tea..."

Angel knew where this was going. Gary would yell for a while, and then unless he got distracted he'd start whaling on Treese. Or Angel.

It gave him a sour feeling in his stomach, but there wasn't anything he could do. He hesitated for only a moment and then with the skill of long practice, Angel slipped sideways through the shadows and around the corner of the building. He broke into a run and cleared the sagging fence in a fear-sharpened leap

The desert spread out before him, reddish gold in the sun, mottled with tufts of grey and green shrubs. He kept on running, loping like a coyote. Behind him, in the distance, he heard Treese cry out once, making him break stride and stumble. Crouching, he clenched his fists and looked back. No sign of Gary. Just the same he sprang up and ran faster. His sharp breathing began to match the pounding of his feet. Dust rose behind him...and then he was alone and free.

ABOUT THE AUTHOR

What if? What if the extraordinary erupts into an ordinary life? A sense of looming adventure, mystery, and magic fuel Susan Brown's imagination and writing, propelling her towards more and more stories for book-lovers who also live in wonder.

Susan lives with her two border collie rescue dogs amid wild woods and overgrown gardens in Snohomish, Washington. From there she supervises her three daughters, assorted sons-in-law and two grandsons. It's a great way to be a writer!

Find more information, free stories,
and news about upcoming books at:
www.susanbrownwrites.com

Susan is also one half of Stephanie Browning, the pen name shared with her writing partner of close to a thousand years, Anne Stephenson.
www.stephaniebrowningromance.com

55720065R00173

Made in the USA
Columbia, SC
17 April 2019